DE

A FRAZIER FALLS NOVEL

KELLY COLLINS

Copyright © 2020 by Kelly Collins
No part of this publication may be reproduced, distributed, or transmitted in any form or by any means, including photocopying, recording, or other electronic or mechanical methods, without the prior written permission of the publisher, except as permitted by U.S. copyright law. For permission requests, contact kelly@authorkellycollins.com.
The story, all names, characters, and incidents portrayed in this production are fictitious. No identification with actual persons (living or deceased), places, buildings, and products is intended or should be inferred. All products or brand names are trademarks of their respective owners.

To every person who has heard mean words and believed them. The wounds we suffer as children hide in our hearts and surface when we least expect it. It's a whisper from your inner child who is still waiting to be defended. Take your younger self in your arms and tell him or her that it's okay to be you.

I would rather be a little nobody, than to be an evil somebody.
Abraham Lincoln

CHAPTER ONE

PAXTON

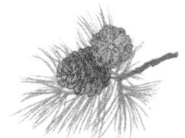

There's a reason we're born with two ears and one mouth. We're supposed to listen more than we talk. If there was one thing I knew with absolute certainty, it was that I learned a whole lot more about what was going on around me if I kept quiet and paid attention.

"Paxton, do you want the usual?" Alice breezed toward me, pad in hand, and a pen sticking out of her poof of hair.

I'd commandeered my brother's booth for the moment, knowing he wasn't going to show up. "Yes, coffee and apple pie, please."

"Coming up." She leaned a hip on the chipped Formica table. "Where are those brothers of yours?"

"Not here."

"Obviously." Alice popped me on the head with her pad and walked away.

My brothers were at Reilly's waiting for me. That's what I wanted to believe, but the reality was they'd be at Reilly's with their significant others and not notice my absence. Their pairing up would leave me the fifth wheel or worse,

Rich's date, which was always awkward because he wasn't my type.

As the youngest brother of the three Coopers, I didn't need to say much, but razzing Alice was a requirement. She was like family and exempt from my silence.

I turned my ears to the chatter surrounding me. Growing up, I enjoyed listening to other people. In most circumstances, someone would always say what I'd been thinking, saving me from voicing my opinion. What was the point of repeating what everyone already knew?

Several people in the diner were discussing my brother Owen and Carla. Their wedding was fast approaching and was the talk of the town. Nothing quite as exciting had happened in Frazier Falls since the avalanche in ninety-seven —eighteen ninety-seven.

The knitting club was crammed into the corner booth betting on the type of flowers they'd have and whether Carl would wear white.

"She's no virgin," Isabel Walker shouted a bit too loudly, which drew the stares of many. She dropped her knitting needles and shook her head.

"Hell, these days, kids are born with experience." Scarlet Lewellen pulled out another ball of yarn and continued her work on what looked like a pair of baby booties. "Miriam's granddaughter is a baby having a baby, and she marched to the altar eight months along and dressed in white."

Wanda Kraft looked over her shoulder at me. "There's one left. Who do you think Paxton will end up with?"

My mouth dropped open. They were talking about me.

"Maybe he'll meet his match at the ceremony."

The entire group turned toward me, and, one by one, they raised their hands and waved.

"Maybe he'll catch the garter, which would mean he'd be next."

I shook my head and made a mental note to avoid the garter at all costs.

"Here you go." Alice slid a plate of pie and a coffee on the table. I swear she always gave me a double portion.

"It's too bad you're taken, Alice. A woman who can make pie like you might be able to enter my heart."

Down came the order pad on my head again. "She's out there waiting for you, Pax. Never say never."

"Never," I said before I shoved my mouth full of pie.

"Someone, someday, will earn their place in your warm, smooshy heart. You're a Teddy bear destined to be hugged and cherished. If you weren't so busy catering to all the widows in town, you might have time to find a woman for yourself."

"I love those cougars." There was nothing going on between me and the senior residents of Frazier Falls. I liked to be helpful and found my niche assisting the older folks of my little town.

"Between work and Lucy Rogers, you may never find a mate. Although, there's a table of interesting women giving you a look over now." We both glanced at the knitters in the corner.

"Not looking for one." I loved the term she used because while I liked the mating part, I wasn't that good at all the rest.

Alice trotted off in her red high-top sneakers, while I reflected on my existence. I enjoyed working with my brothers. Cooper Construction was a successful business, and with Owen's Green House project taking off, we were beginning to garner an excellent reputation across the globe. It was rewarding to do good work and be recognized as an industry leader in green living. Though Owen was the one who designed his eco-friendly houses, I was the one responsible for much of the building of them and the running of the company.

It had always worked well. Owen was the architect, and Eli was the numbers guy. Then, when we got on-site, the responsibility fell to me to ensure the actual construction work got done.

It was the way I liked it. Good, honest, physically hard work left my mind free to wander. It also meant that I never had to take work home like my brothers. My free time was filled by helping others with tasks they couldn't always do themselves. I didn't know when or why I'd started doing this, but it filled me with a deep sense of satisfaction that I didn't get from anything else.

Alice's comment about helping others taking up too much of my time was dead wrong. It was actually a time saver. Because I wouldn't accept compensation, everyone showed their appreciation with homemade food. I might starve if not for Lucy Rogers, Judy Flanagan, and a half dozen others who cooked me casseroles and roasts and baked goods in large quantities.

I finished my pie and laid down a ten to pay before I walked out and headed to the bar to meet my brothers for a beer.

I no sooner walked inside when John Reilly handed me a Tupperware container. "Thank you again for all your help over the winter with the restocking," He nodded toward my brothers and Emily, who sat at the end of the bar. "They're only a half a pint ahead of you."

"I'm a coffee and a piece of pie ahead of them."

"Smart man. Eat before you drink."

I looked down at the gift of food from John. "Irish stew?"

"Yes, with extra carrots just the way you like it."

"You're the best." I tucked the container under my arm and moved toward the group. Carla and her brother Rich hadn't arrived yet.

I glanced at Eli. "I've got Irish stew if you want to join me after our beer."

My brother shook his head and wrapped his arm around his girlfriend's shoulder. "Emily and I already have plans."

"I know what that means," Owen laughed. "They're going to indulge in a different appetite."

"I'm not discussing my sex life with you," Eli muttered. He turned to me before adding, "I'm happy to take that off your hands, though. I'm sure you've got plenty of similar dishes filling your refrigerator and freezer." Eli looked at Emily. "We'll have to come up for air and forage for food at some point."

She gave him a solid slug in the arm. "You said you weren't talking about our sex life."

A smile curled my lips. "Nope, I'll have no problem eating it on my own. Reilly's Irish stew is amazing."

"You pig," Eli called out.

I shrugged my shoulders, indifferent to the insult.

Owen looked at me. "Mind if I steal some for Carla and me?"

"I'll bring it over to your place, and we can share the meal," I said.

Eli pouted. "Why share with him?"

"Because he didn't call me a pig."

"Nope, not out loud anyway," Owen chimed in as Carla and her brother Rich walked into the bar. "That wasn't an invite to join us; it was a request for food."

I slapped a hand over my heart. "I'm wounded."

Carla kissed Owen's cheek as he handed her a beer.

"Pax offered to bring us his dinner. Irish stew, compliments of John."

She looked at the container and me. "Can I take the stew and pass on the visit? I love you brother-to-be, but I've got plans for Owen, and they don't call for a chaperone."

"Geez, I swear you're going to wear yourselves out before the honeymoon." I looked from Owen and Carla to Eli and Emily, trying to make a point. "See what happens when you set a date? It's like a race to the finish and once you're married—"

Emily broke in. "That's why Eli and I have no intention of getting married any time soon. We need lots of practice."

Eli looked at her, "Now who's talking?" He gave me a tap. "I'd say get a girlfriend, so you're not so lonely, but I fear that would be an impossible task."

"Rude." It was true, though. I had dated women in the past, but I'd never had a serious girlfriend before. I didn't want one. Women were … complicated. Often chatty and I wasn't good with expressing my emotions. I didn't say any of this to my present company because I knew that both Emily and Carla would pull my ear for hours explaining the benefits of a girlfriend.

"Pax, get your head back in the conversation," Owen said.

"I was never out of it." I pointed to the group. "Don't forget your roles. You're the talkers; I'm the listener. Want to quiz me? I can repeat anything you've ever told me. Can't answer to the things you haven't."

By their expressions, they knew I was referring to Owen's panic attacks. Particularly the one he had at the architectural exhibit where I discovered that Eli had known about Owen's anxiety problems for years, and I'd been kept in the dark.

Before that, I'd assumed we never spoke about such things because there was nothing to talk about. Now I knew we were all idiots who probably needed to open up to each other more often. "You want a word-by-word retelling?" They knew I could do it. Eli scowled, while the rest of the group laughed.

"Did you have a look at the plans I sent you for the

wedding venue?" Owen abruptly changed the topic of conversation.

I suppressed a scowl. "Yes."

"And …?"

"And that's a hell of a lot of work you want me to do."

"Come on," Owen protested. "You're the only person I know who could build what we need as quickly as we need it."

"No, I'm the only one you know of who will do it for free."

"May as well keep it in the family, right?"

I sighed with resignation.

"You already knew I'd do it, so don't act as if you were giving me a choice."

Carla squealed with delight as she hugged me. "Thanks, Pax. You're a lifesaver."

"Building it on top of the creek will be complicated," I warned. "The design is more elaborate than it needs to be. Simple and sturdy will keep you all dry."

Owen laughed. "I'll keep that in mind."

The rest of the evening passed by in an easy conversation that I was happy to listen to. Aside from a sarcastic comment here and there, I had no need to speak up, which sat perfectly in my lane.

As I leaned back and watched my brothers, I thought about how complicated their lives had become. What used to be a Friday night beer with siblings was now a coordinating of schedules nightmare. We also used to talk about chicks, but now the only topic of conversation was flower choices, types of cake, and tuxedo fittings.

I would happily live my life without those problems.

I left the bar alone, knowing that single was spectacular—or at least that was my story and I was sticking to it.

CHAPTER TWO

ROSE

"You think he's gonna ask you, Rose? Gonna ask you to move in with him?"

"What else can it be? We've been dating for over a year now—it's about time."

Nicolas let out a noise of excitement, wringing his hands in expectation as we made our way down to the graphics department of Flair, the fashion magazine for which we were both working as editors. "I can't believe it's finally happening. And that penthouse of his is … wow. It's out of an interior designer's dream."

"I know, right?" I babbled back, feeling immensely proud of the fact I had managed to find a man with an innate sense of style for both his home and his clothes. Not to mention that James Rivers, the man in question, was absolutely loaded. Not that his money was what had attracted me to him in the first place, but still … it certainly didn't make him any less appealing.

"Where's he taking you tonight? Oh my God, Sandra, this is all wrong," Nick suddenly bit out in response to the proofs given to him for inspection by his assistant. "What's up with the focal point? You know that Franco will destroy you if it isn't off-center. We needed these photos almost two hours ago, and now they'll take even longer."

"I'm sorry, Nick, we have a newbie who made a mistake," Sandra apologized. "We'll get it fixed as soon as possible."

Nick was unhappy. "You put a newbie on something this important? What were you thinking?"

"We're understaffed right now. Dan and Rach are off with the flu, and Denise is on vacation."

"Argh, fine. Prioritize getting them fixed before the end of the day."

Visibly relieved, Sandra said, "Thanks, Nick," before running off.

"You could afford to cut her a little slack, you know," I said to him quietly as we exited the building, heading toward our local Starbucks. "You already knew damn well that the design department is understaffed right now."

"Exactly why there is no slack to be had. This month's edition will be late otherwise."

My breath released quick and loud like a balloon just popped. "I guess so. I must admit it's pretty funny how many people are scared of you when you're younger than most of them."

Nicolas was only twenty-eight—three years younger than me—but he had proven himself to be indispensable to Flair Magazine. I had no doubt he'd end up heading the editorial department by the time he hit thirty.

I had no interest in being the editorial head. I was happy with the simultaneous freedom and responsibility that came with being one of the three senior editors for the magazine. People respected me. They valued my opinion. But I didn't have to spend too much time dealing with arduous pencil-pushing and pointless sweet-talking, instead, getting to dedicate all my time to what I loved best—fashion.

I didn't think I'd gotten a full eight hours of sleep in any given night for at least five years, and there were definitely outfits in my wardrobe that deserved to be burned to a fine ash, but for the most part, I loved my high-flying job in New York City. Sure, it could be stressful, especially when a deadline was coming up, but it was also exciting and addictive. I loved the parties, the dresses, the champagne. I loved the photoshoot locations and choosing the glossy centerfolds beloved by our readers.

And I loved the people I met through my job … most of all, my current boyfriend. Hopefully, after tonight, we'd become something a little more serious. I had never seen myself as the marrying type, but that idea had gone out the window the moment I met James. Our wedding would be the kind of thing that would ignite the fires of jealousy in the hearts of all women.

I thought of getting to choose the dress, the venue, the décor, the alcohol … it would be divine. I'd be able to invite all of my old school friends from Frazier Falls and watch their expressions of disbelief at how successful I'd become in a town that swallowed its inhabitants by the thousands daily. How many dreamers had come to New York only to leave destroyed?

I thought about Carla Stevenson's wedding, which I was going home for in a couple of weeks, and how my own future wedding would be so different. Not better, but different.

"What's that look on your face all about?" Nick asked as he ordered us two cappuccinos. "I'm happy for your blossoming relationship and all, but I won't pretend it doesn't sting to see you nab a guy who has everything when I'm lonely and single."

"Oh, I was thinking about how different my life is from my childhood friends'. It wasn't about you."

"Plan to do some rubbing in your successes when you get home?"

"Of course not. I'm excited to have something to share. Weddings are contagious, you know?"

He walked over and rubbed my arm. "Too bad you aren't a four-leaf clover because I'd stick you in my wallet."

I stuck my tongue out at Nick as we were handed our coffees. "James is already taken. You'll have to find your own man." We took our coffees back to the office because there was no rest for the wicked in our line of work. "In other news, did you know that Dalia from HR interviewed for a job over at Vogue?"

He nodded. "I actually heard from her supervisor this morning that she didn't get it. Bless her tiny little soul. Bet it'll be awkward going back into the office after this."

"How did her supervisor know? I thought she was trying to keep the interview secret until she knew for sure if she got the job?" In five minutes, we were in the elevator heading back to our floor.

Nick leaned in and whispered, despite us being alone. "Her supervisor's sleeping with the head of HR at Vogue."

"No way." My head spun. There were lots of ways to get to the top. Hard work was my plan, but some chose the lazier on-their-back route.

"Yes," he said. "It would seem to me to be a conflict of interest."

I burst out laughing. "Ooh, what an HR scandal."

"Who do you think cleans up the mess when the heads of human resources are the ones in question?"

"I'm not sure, actually," I replied, holding a finger to my chin as I thought on it. "Maybe that's a job for the CEO?"

"I'll get all the dirty details and let you know."

"Don't interrupt my date with James."

The elevator door opened, and we reentered the office.

With a busy afternoon ahead of us, my primping time before meeting James for our date was limited. In ordinary circumstances, this would be less than desirable, but I worked for a fashion magazine, and we got lots of samples.

"Where's the date? Smith & Wollensky's? Per Se?"

"He's taking us to the little late-night café where we first met."

Nick wrinkled his nose. "That sounds underrated but cute."

"I suppose it is. We had both left the same charity fundraiser and bumped into each other at the café. Clearly, we'd had the same sobering-up idea ... coffee and bacon."

"This isn't a dress-up affair."

I flashed him a smile. "We're going to that new bar called Blaze afterward, so it definitely is a dress-up occasion."

"Not fair. I've been trying to get on the guest list for weeks."

"Turns out James' roommate from college is one of the partners, so we got on the list no problem."

He scowled at me. "I don't suppose you thought of poor old me when you found out about this wonderful connection of yours?"

I pulled out my cell phone and showed him the guest list. "I did. Thought I'd surprise you. Got you a plus-one in case you can rummage up a date."

"I'll let that one slide. All I need to do is swipe right," Nick said, his brows waggling. "This is going to make for a great night."

Hours later, with the workday finally finished, Nick helped me decide between a pair of classic stiletto heels or more delicate heeled wedges to pair with my slinky, backless dress. It was midnight blue, and according to Nick, looked amazing against my pale skin and fair hair.

Nick pinched his chin between his thumb and index

finger and frowned. "I get what you're trying to do with the wedges, and it does feel like summer with this unseasonable heat," he mused, "but I think you should go full-on sex queen and choose the stilettos. Keep your hair boho-chic if you want to take the edge off things, but definitely go for the red lipstick."

I slipped on the heels, doing up the clasps on the straps before applying a layer of dark, blood-red lipstick and fluffing up my hair around my face. I blew Nick a kiss as I grabbed my bag and headed for the exit. "Thanks for the second opinion."

"Second? My opinion is the only one that counts," he teased. "Let me know how it goes with Mr. Dream Boat," he called out after me. "Love you."

"Love you more." I did love him. He was an everything guy. My brother. My sister. My best friend. Tonight, he was my personal stylist.

I hailed a cab to take me to the café where I'd first met James Rivers. I resisted the urge to order a coffee as I sat at a rickety outdoor table waiting for him. I checked the time on my cell several times, looking for messages indicating that he'd be late, but there was nothing.

"Odd," I murmured, "he's usually early."

Twenty minutes later, there was still no sign of James. I had sent him a couple of texts which he hadn't responded to, so I risked giving him a call. Again, no response.

Forty minutes later, I was well on my way to a case of nerves. What if something had happened to him? What if he was in the hospital and nobody knew to contact me? Maybe it was simply traffic. I hoped it was the latter. Although, if it was the latter, he should have called.

Over an hour and one terrible espresso later, I had to admit that James wasn't going to show for whatever reason. As I rose from my seat, my phone buzzed. My heart raced with excitement, only to be full of disappointment once more when I saw it was Nick who had messaged me.

Get your ass over here now, the message read. **Unless Mr. Dream Boat has an evil twin, I think there's something you need to see.**

Another buzz of my phone and Nick had sent me a photo from the bar I was supposed to be at.

On my screen was James kissing another woman like his life depended on it.

I got to the bar in under ten minutes, struggling to maintain my composure as I walked up to the doorman and told him my name. He glanced at me, surprised.

"Miss Rose Rogers already entered the premises with Mr. James Rivers, ma'am."

I pulled out my ID and my credit card. "Then someone must be pretending to be me. I'm Rose Rogers."

He looked away uncomfortably, as if he knew something bad was about to happen, but he waved me in, nonetheless.

I locked on to James immediately. It was hard not to, what with his entire body currently entwined with some dark-haired stranger. They were an inch short of copulating on the dance floor. I marched up to them without thinking of what I'd do when I got there.

Out of the corner of my eye, I saw Nick mouthing "destroy him" to me.

I pulled them apart, but James didn't even look surprised.

"Oh hey, Rose," he said, looking as if he was about to return to sucking the face off the woman who stared at me with open animosity.

"What the hell is this?" I waved a hand at the two of them. "You were supposed to meet me at Rico's over an hour ago, and I find you here cheating on me?"

James chuckled. "I didn't mean to forget. I'm sorry. I've

been drinking with my work friends since lunchtime. Forgive me?"

"Forgive you?" I reached up to wipe the red lipstick from his lips. "This should be mine!"

"James, who is this?" The dark-haired stranger sounded agitated.

I turned on her. "Who am I? I'm his girlfriend. Who are you?"

The woman's head snapped back as if she'd been slapped. "You never mentioned a girlfriend."

"We're not exclusive," he said, waving a hand dismissively.

"We're ... *what?*"

James looked uncomfortable. "Rosie, don't make a scene. We can talk about this—"

"Don't you dismiss me!" I screamed. "I was thinking you were going to ask me to move in with you and then—"

He held up a five-finger stop sign. "Wait, hold on. What on earth made you think that?"

I glanced around the room at everyone watching us. Part of me knew it would be better to take the high ground and walk away gracefully. This was something that should be discussed in private. The wounded part of me wanted an answer now.

"What has this past year been to you? Was I simply a place-holder girlfriend you could introduce to your mom and dad and your boss while you snuck around with other women behind my back?"

"Rosie, it's more complicated than that ..."

I grabbed the closest drink I could find, which happened to be a martini held by a woman nearby, and I threw it at him.

"We're done!"

He didn't even run after me. Nick did. Now I had to add

savior to his list of titles. He'd spared me from the biggest mistake of my life.

"Oh my God, Rose, I'm so sorry."

"Don't be."

He continued to rush after me as I hailed a cab, and he grabbed my arm before I got in one. "Where are you going?"

"Home."

"Rose, you live, like, five minutes from here."

"I mean *home,* home."

"Frazier Falls?"

"I have use or lose days I need to take, so consider this an extended, overdue vacation."

Nick looked conflicted. "Are you sure you should go feeling like this?"

I gave him a quick hug before flinging myself inside the cab.

"When you start at the bottom, there's only one direction to travel." How could I possibly feel worse than I did now? Even returning to Frazier Falls was an upgrade to my current situation.

Once I got there, I'd forget about James freaking Rivers entirely—or so I hoped. I'd run from Frazier Falls years ago to prove I was more, and now I was returning feeling like less.

CHAPTER THREE

PAXTON

"Who'd have thought after the awful winter we had we'd get such a warm spring, Paxton?" Lucy folded herself, heels and all, into the plush furniture on the deck. She held her wine like a cup of tea with a pointed pinky out to the side.

"I suppose we shouldn't complain. Wouldn't want to jinx it."

"No, but it's wonderful to be able to use my garden right off the bat. Though I'm sorry to drag you over to mow the lawn so soon after the last time—all this sunshine has the grass growing like nobody's business."

I smiled as I wiped the back of my hand across my forehead, mopping the sweat from my brow. It was warm for May. The kind of warm that came with fireworks, picnics, watermelon, and cold beer. "It's not a problem, Lucy. I wasn't doing anything, anyway."

"Oh, that makes me feel worse." The pout was fake, but it was her. Seemed to be a family trait. "I'm taking up all your free time."

Lucy Rogers was in her early fifties and didn't look a day

over forty-five. She was more than capable of looking after herself, but when her husband suddenly died almost three years ago, I found myself stepping in to help her out with everything he'd done around the house. Though I was well aware that she had taken to abusing this, I didn't mind. She was an excellent cook.

"Do you have plans for the rest of the afternoon?" I asked politely as I readied the lawnmower. It needed maintenance, so I made a mental note to bring motor oil from the office the next time I came around.

"All I plan to do is sit here and enjoy a nice glass of wine while a young, handsome man cleans up my garden." She held up the glass and made herself comfortable on the outdoor sofa. It was part of an elaborate outdoor furniture set that she had spent a small fortune on. "Who needs an all-male review when I've got a private show each time you mow my lawn?"

"I might begin to suspect you're objectifying me, Mrs. Rogers."

"I never." She held her hand against her heart in mock horror. "I'm a perfect lady, Mr. Cooper. Tell me a time when I've shoved a dollar in your pants."

"I have no use for dollars, but that pasta you made last week was amazing."

I plucked a few weeds from the garden while Lucy idly chatted away.

"Three weeks until Owen and Carla's big day. You must be getting excited for them, no?"

"If they didn't have me building a stage for them on the creek that would need dismantling the next day, then yes."

"I'm sure that's no problem for you. You're a strapping young lad."

Lucy's compliments were often piled on rather high.

"I'm sure he'll pay you back in kind when it's your turn to get married."

I let out a bark of laughter, which I entirely failed to turn into a cough.

Lucy frowned. "What's so funny?"

"Nothing," I murmured. "Don't see myself getting a girlfriend, let alone getting married."

"Ah, you Cooper brothers are all the same. Were Owen and Eli not exactly like you before they met Carla and Emily? And now look at them. Two fools in love if ever I saw them. I remember when my Rupert used to look at me like that—even after I turned forty. That was true love right there." Her wistful sigh filled the air.

How awful to have loved and lost. Sadness pricked at my heart. The loss of a loved one was profound. It ate at a person's soul bit by bit. I remembered how my mother and father used to look at each other, and how lost my father had been when Mom died. It was as if he no longer had the will to live, despite having three sons who desperately hoped he'd make a recovery.

He never did, not until the day he died. That was the first day we'd seen him look peaceful since Mom had passed away. I wasn't the religious type, but even I had to admit that the idea of my parents reuniting in some kind of afterlife was a wonderful thing.

"How long were the two of you together?"

She looked over at me, surprised by the question. I rarely asked such personal things. She smiled as the memory seemed to wash over her. "I met him in college. It was love at first sight. Everyone thought I was ridiculous, getting pregnant with a man I barely knew at twenty, but I'd never been surer of anything in my life. I wanted Rupert's baby, and I wanted us to be a family."

This was why I stayed quiet and listened. There was so much to learn and take in. "I bet you were a looker too."

Lucy sipped her wine. I didn't know if the blush on her cheeks was from the alcohol or the compliment.

"I finished college because an education is important," she happily rambled on now that I'd gotten her started. "My father would've never forgiven me if I hadn't. It was tough being pregnant in my senior year, but I managed it. Even managed to graduate early. That may have been more to do with the fact I couldn't go out partying with my friends due to the pregnancy."

"When did the two of you marry?"

"Not until little Rosie was five. We didn't have a lot of money, and we wanted it to be special. You don't remember it, Paxton? Your parents brought all you Cooper boys along to the reception."

"I don't remember at all," I lied smoothly.

In truth, I tended to blank out anything and everything concerning her daughter, Rose. Even at the age of five, she had picked on me. Her bullying had only gotten worse when we reached middle school. It was in high school that she finally grew bored of it and left me alone.

That was a godsend given that I had Brady Huck to deal with. That was another matter altogether.

"I suppose it was thirty years ago."

"Twenty-six," I corrected. "Don't make me feel even older than I already am."

"How old do you think it makes me feel?" she laughed. "I'm a widow, and I have a grown daughter."

"You don't look a day over forty-two, and you know it."

"Oh, you spoil me too much. I tell you what, young man. Give up on this silly notion that you don't need a girlfriend. My Rosie is coming back to town in a couple of weeks for your brother's wedding. She was always such good friends with Carla back in the day." She moved her hand through the air as if she was directing a symphony. "Lord knows what a fashion-conscious cheerleader and the biggest tomboy in Frazier Falls had in common, but they hit it off regardless. Maybe you and Rosie should go on a date."

Her eyes grew as round and large as dinner plates while she considered the idea. It wasn't the first time she'd brought it up. I didn't have the heart to tell her that, out of all the women in all the world, the last one I would choose to go on a date with would be her daughter.

"She has her own life in New York," I replied, carefully avoiding answering Lucy's suggestion. "Doesn't she have a boyfriend? Jake or Jack or whatever."

"Oh, you mean James?" I knew it was James, but I didn't care. "I'm surprised you remembered me mentioning him before."

"Only vaguely. You haven't said anything about them breaking up, so I'm assuming they must still be going strong."

Her face twisted into a grimace. "Truth be told, I hope it doesn't last. I don't know why I don't like him when I haven't even met him, but I don't."

"I'm sure he's great." It would serve Rose right if he was a selfish, arrogant ass. Karma was a bitch, and a bad boyfriend would be the least she deserved. That was harsh since I didn't actually wish anything but kindness on Rose and her family, but even I could admit that old wounds healed slowly.

"I guess I'll see him at the wedding. Rose is being coy about whether she's bringing him, but she did say she'd be bringing a plus-one."

"Great." I started the lawnmower's engine, happily cutting off the topic of conversation about her daughter. I didn't want to think about her, much less talk about her to her mother. At least if the topic of Rose were to come up with my brothers, they would understand my less than amicable feelings.

I lined up the wheels so the stripes left behind were perfectly spaced and straight. I liked order in my life. The thought of Rose's visit sent things into chaos. Lucy said her daughter was returning in two weeks, which meant she'd be back for nine or ten days. I resisted the urge to scowl. She would be with Carla, which meant I'd have to spend time with her acting cordial. I didn't think I had it in me. I could simply remain silent, since that's what she was used to, anyway.

My pace picked up when I decided to use my silence against her. I settled into a contented rhythm in order to cut the grass, humming tunelessly along with the thrum of the engine as I worked.

Fifteen minutes later, I'd sweated through my T-shirt. Despite knowing exactly how Lucy would react, I pulled it off with one fluid movement, relishing the feel of the sun on my back.

"Now, that's the spirit." Lucy lifted her wine glass and shouted over the growl of the lawnmower.

A flash of yellow drew my attention to the street when a cab pulled up in front of her house. She stood and squinted against the sun, watching the car in confusion. Clearly, she hadn't been expecting anyone.

When an annoyingly familiar head of blond hair popped out of the rear passenger door, I turned the lawnmower around in an attempt to finish cutting the grass as quickly as possible.

"God, Mom, am I glad to see you," Rose called out to her mother loud enough to be heard over the roar of the lawnmower. I wished it could have been louder. Loud enough to drown her out completely.

Of all the people I didn't want to see, it was the woman now unabashedly staring at me.

She frowned before her eyes widened in recognition.

"Paxton?"

I'd never wanted to be involved in a freak lawnmower accident more than in that moment.

CHAPTER FOUR

ROSE

The fact that my mom had hired someone to mow the lawn came as no surprise to me. After all, it's not like I would have expected her to do it, with her perfectly dyed peroxide blonde hair, immaculate manicure, and obscenely high heels. The fact that the man in question was shirtless and undeniably a complete and utter babe wasn't all that surprising either, considering the new lease on life that had filled Mom after months of grieving for Dad. She was allowed to have her eye-candy.

What was the most surprising thing was that said eye-candy looked disturbingly familiar.

My mind immediately went to Owen Cooper, but after gawking at the man for a few seconds, I realized that wasn't quite right.

"Paxton?" I called out again over the dull roar of the lawnmower. "Paxton Cooper? Is that you?"

He ignored me and continued to cut the grass as if I hadn't shown up at all. Maybe he hadn't heard me.

I grabbed my bag out of the trunk of the taxi before paying the fare and rushing up the stone steps to crush my mother in a massive hug. Now that the shock had worn off from me arriving two weeks early, she made a noise of delight and hugged me tighter in return.

"Oh, Rosie, what a nice surprise. I wasn't expecting you until the twenty-first."

"Plans change, and I had vacation days stacked up. Figured I'd take an extra two weeks off. We haven't had a chance to catch up in months." I wasn't ready to tell her I'd been dumped. I'd cried the entire flight and was out of tears for James Rivers.

"Years, more like, given how hectic your schedule is. I haven't seen you for longer than three consecutive days since your father died."

I felt a pang of guilt. It was my fault I hadn't taken time off. I smiled, a little sadly. "I'm here now. Time to make up for all that."

Mom glanced at my bag as she raised a dubious eyebrow. "You packed rather light for a three-week trip."

"I may have left New York on short notice," I said, laughing awkwardly. "Nick is going to send more stuff along for me, and I've ordered some new clothes that should arrive here tomorrow."

"It's a wonder what you can do with the internet these days," Mom remarked, genuinely astounded. "If you see something you like on a screen, all you have to do is click a button, and it's there the next day, even here in Frazier Falls."

I made a face. "Actually, it takes two days to reach Frazier Falls. I ordered the clothes yesterday when I was waiting for a flight."

"You've been in the airport since yesterday? Honey, what happened?"

Her words came out as an overwhelming shout as the sound of the lawnmower was cut off. I was immediately reminded that Paxton was there and turned to face him.

"Paxton, sweetheart," Mom simpered, "come over here. Can you believe Rosie came home early to surprise me?"

"Mom, stop calling me Rosie. I'm an adult."

He looked at the two of us for a moment, then indicated with a wave of his hand that he was going to put the lawnmower away in the shed.

I glanced at my mom. "When did he get so buff?" For a second, a long time ago, I had a secret crush on Paxton, the boy. But wow, he'd grown up to become quite a good looking man.

"Oh, that's right. You haven't seen him since before you left for college, have you?"

I shook my head.

"He was a bit of a late-bloomer compared to his older brothers, but maybe that's because he was a much smaller baby. Either way, when he returned, he was the spitting image of his mom poured into his brothers' bodies. Although, I must admit, he's possibly even more handsome than all the other Coopers." She lifted her shoulders. "I might be biased."

I narrowed my eyes. "How often does he cut the grass for you?"

"He doesn't only mow the lawn, Rose. He's such an angel. He's been helping me with everything since your father died. I mean, he pretty much helps out everyone in town, but he has a soft spot for me. He spoils me too much … not that I'm complaining." She seemed incredibly pleased with this fact.

I couldn't imagine gawkish, silent Paxton Cooper being capable of helping anyone, much less my mom. I'd never heard him string more than a few words together, and even then, it'd seemed like it pained him to do so.

And yet, the grown-up him looked a world away from how he had looked as a teenager. Maybe he had finally figured out that normal people conversed with one another.

With what looked like obvious reluctance, the man in question walked over to join us after he had put away the lawnmower. His gaze swept over me quickly before he turned his attention to my mom. I became acutely aware that I was still wearing my backless blue dress and heels, which was entirely inappropriate attire for having flown all the way from New York.

"Paxton, you remember my daughter Rose," my mother said excitedly. "Sure, you do. You went to school together."

"I was in the year below," I said. "It's not as if we had classes together."

Clearly, Paxton had never gotten around to telling my mom that I incessantly teased him all the way through middle school, and he no doubt hated me. Then again, I couldn't imagine him speaking for long enough to tell her anything.

He inclined his head in lieu of an answer, which pissed me off for some reason.

"Oh, before I forget, I made you an Asian stir fry," my mom said. "I know how much you like it. I'll go and grab it from the kitchen. Be a love and keep him company while I'm gone, Rosie."

She gave me a not-so-subtle look that screamed *he is definitely dating material*. It made me want to laugh because the last thing Nick said before I left was the best way to get over one man was to get under another. Having hours to think about James and my relationship, I realized we hadn't really had one. He was always gone, and I was the on-call friend with benefits.

When she left, I eyed him critically. He had filled out his tall frame. He was all taut muscles and broad shoulders. The fact that he was still shirtless with the sunlight accentuating his abs drove home the fact that he was drop-dead gorgeous and front-cover worthy.

And his face ... he'd always had beautiful eyes. As a middle-schooler, a boy having beautiful eyes was a reason to tease him, rather than adore him. I had done both.

A classic five o'clock shadow covered his perfect jawline while his thick hair was pushed back to keep it out of his eyes. Thirty-two-year-old Paxton Cooper was quite possibly the most handsome man I had ever met in my life.

James who? I couldn't help but ask. Although my heart still hurt at the betrayal, my mind was firmly in the "move on" camp. Wasn't that what James had done? Life was short, and I certainly wasn't going to waste more time on a man who didn't love me.

Paxton's face was expressionless as he muttered, "Are you done?"

My eyes widened in shock. Not only had he spoken, but presumably, he meant to insult my obvious ogling.

"What do you mean by that?" I fired back.

He didn't respond. Instead, he walked away and picked up his T-shirt from where it lay abandoned on the grass. He then sat on the edge of my mom's outdoor couch and pulled out his cell phone. He proceeded to scroll through it as if he were checking his emails or social media.

I couldn't decide whether those three words were all he had, or if he was deliberately ignoring me. I walked over to his side, putting my hand in front of his cell phone screen so he couldn't see it. "Aren't you even going to say hello?"

He glanced up at me, his face still devoid of emotion, but he said nothing.

"God, you're so weird," I said, frustrated, before pulling my hand away and heading inside the house.

When I passed Mom in the hallway, she looked stricken. "Why have you left Paxton alone?"

"I'm tired, Mom. I went through a horrible break up, and I'm not in the mood to talk to old friends yet." It wasn't entirely a lie. In fact, the only part that was truly a lie was the friend part.

She looked at me sympathetically. "Let me see him off, and you can tell me all about it."

When I reached my childhood bedroom, I collapsed onto my mattress in relief. Even though I had desperately wanted to leave Frazier Falls, I still loved this house. So many good memories had been created here with my family.

Exhaustion overwhelmed me, but my desire to get out of my clothes and into something clean was stronger. I quickly stripped off the dress and ran a brush through my hair before I headed for a shower. The hot water raced over my skin, clearing away the hurt seeping from my pores. But it felt different, and I had to wonder if my hurt was now because of Paxton's complete dismissal. I stayed in the shower for far longer than was required, probably hoping that I could scrub away all the painful memories, both past and present.

Eventually, I had to get out. Toweling myself dry, I located an old, oversized T-shirt and some shorts I hadn't worn since I was seventeen. I was somewhat satisfied that they still fit me. A little horrified that Mom had kept them, along with my Dalmatian pajamas and my posters of the cast of Glee.

I found Mom in the kitchen, pouring another glass of wine. Wordlessly she passed it over to me before pouring a new one for herself.

"Thanks," I said, appreciating the gesture.

She glanced at my clothes. "You'd never have been caught dead in public wearing a T-shirt like that back in high school."

I laughed. "No, but I wore them around the house." I looked down at my Lady Gaga T-shirt. "I'll have new clothes tomorrow, so for now, this is okay."

"What happened with your boyfriend?"

I lifted my shoulders in a shrug, hoping my indifference would limit the conversation. "I thought things were going well. I thought wrong."

"I take it he broke up with you?" She reached out her hand and cupped my cheek in the way moms do when they think their daughter is headed for a meltdown.

I shook my head. "No, I broke up with him. I found him cheating on me, though he claimed we were never exclusive. Lying bastard. I was always exclusive."

"This is why you need an honest, straight-forward kind of man, not any of these smarmy city-slicker types. Like, oh, I don't know …"

"Don't you dare say Paxton, Mom."

She looked offended. "What's wrong with him?"

"Nothing. I need a break from guys for a while. You understand that, right?" I wasn't going to tell her that Paxton and I were like putting a cat and bird in a cage. While I might find him reasonably attractive, we weren't a good match.

She pouted. "What about your plus-one for Carla's wedding?"

"I'll invite Nick. He'll be ecstatic to finally visit my hometown."

"Is he handsome?" Mom asked, her pink slicked lips growing wide with a smile.

"Yes," I laughed, "and decidedly gay."

"Hmm, I've always wondered about Carla's brother, you know. Maybe we could try setting them up at the wedding. Rich is a good-looking man."

"Oh, give it a rest. I can't imagine how horrified Rich would be if you did that."

"We won't know unless we try."

It wasn't actually a terrible idea. If Rich wasn't straight, what was the harm? I'd have to ask Carla. I didn't know, and

I wasn't one to assume everyone I knew was straight these days, especially given the industry I worked in.

"On that incredibly disturbing note," I joked, downing my wine in the process, "I'm going to get some sleep. I haven't been in a bed in forty-eight hours. I need to crash."

Mom smiled as I left the kitchen and made for the stairs. "Sleep well, Rosie."

When I reached my bedroom, she called up to me, "And maybe consider meeting with Paxton for a coffee while you're here. It wouldn't hurt."

I answered the suggestion by closing my door rather loudly.

"Wouldn't hurt my ass," I grumbled as I burrowed under the soft duvet. "It'd be like sitting with a rock to discuss world hunger. Nothing would get said, and everyone would still starve."

CHAPTER FIVE

PAXTON

I thought about Rose again, and I didn't want to. Her showing up when she did threw me off. Carla and Owen's wedding was still three weeks away. Why on earth had she taken that much time off work?

Being curious about her even to that degree was going too far, so I shrugged the matter off and focused on Rich.

We were drinking in Reilly's; our siblings were on dates with their significant others. It still felt strange to be missing both of my brothers on a Friday night. We'd spent them together for so long now that I'd forgotten what it felt like to not have them around.

I stared up at the message of the day. John Reilly spread his Zen from a chalkboard. Today's saying was one from someone named Tosso. *Any time not spent on love is wasted.* I was ready to waste some time.

"Is tonight a beer or a spirits night, Pax?" Rich murmured into his empty glass.

"Well, you're already on your third vodka, so I'd wager spirits."

He waved a hand dismissively. "As if that matters. It's not as fun to drink without the group here."

"I'm so glad you hate my company so much."

"Hey, you know that you completely buckle if you have to start and lead a conversation. It's not my fault that you're not a talker."

I raised an eyebrow. "I thought controlling a conversation was your strength?"

"I'm allowed an off-day once in a while. I think I'd rather listen to people speak than do the gabbing myself tonight."

Behind the bar, Ruth McCall laughed.

"Rich, you're not in the mood to talk? You haven't shut up since you beat the gizzard out of Owen right over there a few months ago." She nodded to where the fight between Owen and Rich had taken place. A fight that could and did change the trajectory of all their lives.

"I'd rather forget that night, but my sister won't let me." He lifted his glass. "Another please, Ruthie, but can you add some cranberry juice?"

She shook her head as she laughed. "Remember to pace yourself."

"Since when do you drink vodka cranberries?" I asked. "I thought only Owen tossed down the girlie stuff."

He shrugged. "What can I say? They've grown on me."

"I'm not touching that sugary crap. Could I have a whiskey, Ruthie?"

She beamed at me. "You bet. On the rocks?"

I considered the question. "No. Make it neat, and a double."

"Should I be concerned about you pacing yourself?"

"Rich is a lightweight. I'm not."

"Fair point." She lifted the Bushmills bottle and let it waterfall into the tumbler below.

Rich rested his head on one fist, elbow glued to the bar, looking at me curiously.

"What happened?"

"Why do you think something happened?"

"I don't know. You seem off."

I supposed I couldn't be all that surprised by Rich noticing I was out of sorts. He'd become like the fourth brother in the Cooper family.

Sighing, I downed some of my whiskey before telling him, "Rose is back in town."

"Well, you knew that would be inevitable given the fact that my sister is the one getting married, and they were best friends."

"Yeah, but what made her come back two weeks early? Lucy told me she wasn't due home until the twenty-first."

"What's your beef with Rose?"

"Let's say we have a long, braided history of dislike for one another."

"Can't you avoid her as much as possible?" he asked. "I mean, we have tons of work to do right now. It shouldn't be too difficult to stay away from her until a few days before the wedding."

"I already ran into her."

Rich frowned. "You want me to hold her down so you can yank her ponytails?"

I chuckled at his childish comeback because that's where he and Rosie left it back in middle school. "She seemed surprised that I'd actually grown up. But then I ignored her."

"You ignored her?"

I nodded. "Figured I can play up the whole no talking thing for a while before she catches on that I'm only ignoring her."

Rich burst out laughing. "I've got to hand it to you, that's pretty genius. She won't understand what's going on when she sees you talking to Carl and Ruthie and Emily like it's no big deal."

"Someone say my name?" Ruth asked, coming over to see what we wanted.

"Nah, it's nothing," Rich said. "Rose Rogers is back, and he's planning to mess with her head a little."

"Rose is Lucy's daughter, yeah?" She cocked her head to the right. "What did this Rose girl do to deserve you messing with her, Pax?"

"She—"

"I asked Paxton, not you, Rich," Ruth interrupted. "I thought you said you weren't in the mood to talk, anyway?"

He laughed apologetically. "Sorry. It seems like everyone steps in to speak for Pax."

Ruth looked at me expectantly. She was too young to have known what I was like back in school, and I liked that. Some reputations were hard to get past. "I barely spoke a word to anyone when I was growing up. Don't ask me why. I simply didn't. Rose bullied me for it until we entered high school."

Her face was plastered with disbelief. "Someone bullied you? A girl, no less. How on earth did that happen?"

"I was a late bloomer," I explained. "I got tall quickly, but nothing else caught up until the summer before college. I was a gawkish, awkward kid who'd rather read than talk. That reputation has followed me around for years. Everyone called me names like weirdo and mute."

Rich glanced at Ruth. "In all fairness, Pax is being hard on himself. He may not have talked much, but I'm certain he wasn't weird. I'd rather read a good mystery than talk to most people."

She narrowed her eyes. "And this Rose girl bullied you for it?"

I nodded. "It was a lifetime ago. I'd rather let it go."

Her eyes flashed. "So how are you getting back at her now that she's in town?"

"He's gonna keep up the silent act in front of her, so she thinks he hasn't changed, then she'll be confused as hell when everyone around him loves him."

"Childish, but I like it," she said, grinning wickedly. "Mind if I join in? I wouldn't mind flirting outrageously with you to mess with her head. Make her think you're a real catch."

"Hey, I am a real catch. Just don't want to be caught." I couldn't help but grin right back. "Either way, your support is appreciated."

"John would kill me if I didn't support the man who helped get us through that horrible winter weather. And you're the least terrible Cooper brother, so you have that going for you."

Rich looked affronted. "Hey, I'm not a Cooper, but there's nothing wrong with me. I'm still in good shape and have all my hair. I'd say I'm still as handsome as I was ten years ago. I'm quite the catch too. Now only to attract my type."

"I was still in high school when you were in college. It would be weird for me to comment on this."

"Aw, so you never had a girly, teenage crush on an older man when you were in high school?" I asked.

She rolled her eyes and looked at me. "Yeah, on your brother Owen."

"But he's the same age as me," Rich said. "And twelve years older than you."

"Yes, and he was an architect and had the dark hair and blue eyes thing going on. Way more my type."

"Until you found out he was a useless idiot, that is." I swirled the brown liquid around my glass.

"Yes. He crushed the teenage me with the reality of who he is," she said with dramatic flair. "Although, to be fair, if he treated me the way he treats Carla, I'd be in heaven. I wasn't the right woman for him." She sighed and looked at Rich. "Your sister was." She switched out Rich's wet napkin for a dry one.

"Have you considered leaving Frazier Falls? You know … fish from a different creek?" I asked.

She looked at me, as surprised as Lucy had been when I'd asked her when she got married. She blushed a little as she looked away.

"Sometimes, but I like it here. This is home, and the people are family."

"Yeah," I laughed. "Inbreeding is still illegal."

She pulled an ice cube from the bin and tossed it at me. "I can't help but sometimes feel like I'm stuck here, and that I should go see the world, but what then? I know me, and I'd only want to come back home."

"The rest of the world is overrated," I tossed back.

"Says the guy who didn't even leave the state for college." Rich sank straight into the Cooper quicksand. He was sinking in deep into our family unit. There wasn't much he didn't know about us, but the tables weren't reversed. While he was learning about everyone else, he didn't divulge much about himself.

"What can I say?" I shrugged. "I'm a creature of habit."

Ruth burst out laughing. "Paxton, you should speak more often. You're kind of cute when you do."

"Cuter when he's not so chatty," Rich added. "Talks straight through movies. Annoying as hell."

"Who visits who all the time?" I turned toward him. Since I couldn't get my brothers to come up for air, I was forced to hang out with Rich. It wasn't a punishment as the guy was cool, but there was no way I was taking the heat for being the needy one in this relationship.

He slung his arm around my shoulders and gave it a squeeze. "Aww, don't be like that. You know you love me."

I gave him a sideways glance. "How are you drunk already?"

"I'm not."

"Ruth, does this look like a drunk man to you?" I asked her, pointing at Rich with my thumb.

"Definitely drunk."

"Hey, that hurts." He swayed in his seat. "I thought you had my back."

"The only time I'm touching your back is when I shove you out the door." I tossed back a gulp.

Ruth was distracted by another customer signaling for attention at the bar, so she excused herself to serve them. Rich let go of me, returning to his previous slouching, head-on-fist-on-table position. He looked at me, uncharacteristically serious.

"You're okay, though, right?"

I frowned. "Why wouldn't I be?"

"I heard she made you cry."

I shifted my feet uncomfortably. "My brothers are telling too many stories. Besides, we were twelve."

"That's not what I heard. Those stories follow you to thirteen, fourteen, and—"

"I get it. But she left me alone when we got into high school, so it's all good."

"Yeah, and then Brady Huck happened," Rich grumbled. "Prick. Why didn't you tell Eli and Owen about the full extent of that? Even Carla knew he bothered you for almost all of your junior year."

I shrugged. "Why didn't Owen tell anyone about his panic attacks? Because he was embarrassed. Why would I bother them with high school drama? They'd already lived it on their own."

"I'd say it was a little more serious than high school drama. I'm sorry you had a terrible adolescence."

"It's high school. Was yours much better?"

Rich let out a chuckle. "Can't say I'd go back again. High school sucked."

"Let's leave it in the past."

By the time I returned home with a drunk Rich in tow, I was thoroughly ready to crash. Rich threw himself on the couch despite the fact I had a spare room and was asleep in seconds. I got him a glass of water and some painkillers, placing them on the coffee table to find in the morning.

After I stripped off my clothes and got into bed, I couldn't help but search for the high school photos someone had recently posted to social media in order to make fun of Carla's tomboy years in preparation for her wedding. It was easy to spot myself in the back row of one.

I was the one that looked like he wanted to melt into the wall. I always stood as far away from Brady Huck as I could.

In the front row was Rose. Our high school had been so small that all classes took photos together, which annoyed me only because of her. She was dressed in her cheerleader uniform, with perfect red lips and her long, sandy-colored hair tied up high in a ponytail. I remember it swishing from side to side as she walked down the school's corridor.

"Face of the devil," I said, turning off my cell phone screen and abandoning it on my bedside table.

There was no denying that Rose had been a beautiful girl, but what was frustrating was how she had somehow gotten even better looking. How she flew from New York in heels, a backless dress, and that ever-present red lipstick still perfectly in place was beyond me, but damn if she didn't look great.

"A bitch is still a bitch," I murmured, not feeling the least bit bad for saying something so brutal.

If there was one person I was allowed to hate until the end of my days, it was Rose.

CHAPTER SIX

ROSE

"Carla."

I rushed in to give my old friend a crushing hug. We hadn't seen each other for a few years, and catching up was long overdue.

"What's it been, like, four years?" she asked, grinning as she messed up my hair, and I shied away from the action.

"Five, actually. Stop acting like my big brother or something. You're only a year older than me, and you're a woman, for goodness' sake."

"I was a woman back then too," she countered, taking her hand back as we strolled along Main Street in Frazier Falls.

"Yeah, but you were such a tomboy. It felt natural, especially with everyone calling you Carl and mistaking you for a guy half the time. "Now it feels weird. It's like you are my mother or big sister since you are older and wearing a dress and makeup. Your hair is even brushed and styled."

She let out a laugh the way some men let out a burp. Loud and unexpected. "I suppose I didn't care much for my appearance back then, did I?"

"Not in the slightest."

"At least now we don't look so out of place next to each other."

I had to hand it to her—she had finally developed a sense of style I could get behind. Her long, wavy, dark brown hair hung loosely around her face, cascading down her back. Her green off-the-shoulder dress hugged her figure where it cinched in at the waist, and floated out around the skirt. Her legs were so long she didn't need to wear heels. I would have been envious if I wasn't so damn happy for her; to snag a man and a Cooper at that.

Thankfully, my new clothes had arrived, so I wasn't stuck in pajamas or that backless blue dress. Donning a gypsy-style outfit and heeled ankle boots, I resembled a woman on-trend. Appearances had always been important to me. Not sure why, but somehow my value was connected to other's opinions.

"Did you dress up for me, or do you dress like this all the time?" Seeing her look feminine was an odd sensation. It reminded me that everyone grew up and changed—had I?

"I'm still in my favorite oil-stained overalls when I'm working at the mill, but it's all dresses and styled hair the rest of the time. Most of my work involves speaking in professional settings now. I'm the face and voice of the Green House Project."

"I can't believe how well you and Owen have been doing this past year—both in business and personally. That was fast."

She rolled her eyes. "I don't care if it seems fast. The two of us knew. Owen is the last person anyone in Frazier Falls would've pegged as a 'he knew' kind of person, but he did, and neither of us wanted to waste more time. We have lives to live and love to share."

Happiness looked good on my friend. Love did crazy shit to people. In Carla's case, it made her wear makeup and dress better. Seeing how beautiful she was now, made me thankful she hadn't taken an interest in girlie things before. Instead of a friend, I would have had a rival.

"I wasn't judging," I replied, though, in truth, I had been. It was warmer in Frazier Falls than it was in New York. A bead of sweat ran down my forehead, so we detoured into Sugar's Sweet Shop to buy an ice cream. "I couldn't believe I got your invitation to be one of your bridesmaids."

"As you pointed out, I was an odd bird and had a small circle of friends. You were definitely top of my list."

"Only one on your list."

"Not true. I could have asked Alice Bransen or Judy Flanagan."

"True, but you'd have to allow for those red Converses from Alice and the whir of the oxygen tank from Judy. Both accessories hard to work around if you had a specific theme in mind."

"Always the fashionista. Weren't you with someone this past year?" she asked. "James or Jack or something?"

"Um, James. We broke up. I caught him cheating on me."

"Ouch." She looked at the ice cream case in front of us, moving right to left to take in all the flavors.

"He said that we were never exclusive. What he meant was he was never exclusive. I've always been a one-man woman."

She scrunched her nose. "That's even worse."

"I know, right? Complete scum bag."

"Good to see you're handling it well." She laughed before turning to the counter in Sugar's to order. "Hey, Sugar, can I have a double salted caramel and chocolate fudge cone, and —" Carla looked at me.

"A single strawberry cone for me, please." I shook my head. "I don't understand where you put all those calories. You've been addicted to sugar ever since you were a kid." I remembered her mom giving her a dollar to get milk at the store, and she'd buy a bag of penny candy with it. Fifty pieces of pure sugar she'd eat before she made it home.

"Hard labor at the mill keeps me in shape. I should watch what I eat now that I spend more time in meetings, but the weather is improving, and I can swim in the creek with Owen, among other things." A dreamy expression floated across her face.

"I bet it's the other things you really enjoy. You don't really swim in the creek, do you? That's your strange metaphor for something else, right?"

With our cones in our hands, we made our way back onto the hot sidewalk, moving toward the park.

"We do. The first dip in the water happened when we were drunk," she replied, eyes hungrily examining where to lick her ice cream first. "But after that, it was for fun and exercise. That pool under the falls is the best. Sometimes I race him to the bend, but I always win. He says he lets me."

"That's cute."

As soon as the words came out, they sounded like a déjà vu moment. Hadn't Nick said something similar before my failed date with James?

Clearly, my breakup had made me cynical, and innocent words became daggers to my soul, not good form in the run-up to Carla's wedding.

"I don't care if it's cheesy or not; we enjoy ourselves."

"I have no doubt." My tongue flicked out to catch the melting ice cream before it ran down the cone. "Tell me ... what's he like in the bedroom?"

Carla choked in response. "What?"

"Aww, come on, we're not in high school. This is grown-up girl talk."

She smiled, and a hint of pink colored her cheeks. "What

do you think?" she said suggestively. "He's well-built and strong and tall and—"

"Okay, okay, maybe I don't want to know. Jealousy was never a good color on me." I laughed. "What you're alluding to is he's a great lay."

"That's a crude way to put it."

"Doesn't make it any less true." I'd been gone so long, and there was a lot to catch up on. I was going to get all the latest gossip I could from her. "I heard Eli recently got a girlfriend."

"He did. Emily's great. She's Irish and judgmental as hell, just like him. She spent the last fifteen years living in California, so she's still adjusting to life here. I think you'd like her."

I smiled. She definitely sounded like someone I could get along with. Anyone with enough patience to deal with a Cooper was good in my book. "It sounds like the Cooper brothers are slowly but surely getting tied down. Never thought I'd see the day."

"Yep, that leaves Pax as the last one standing. Means he's next," Carla said.

We reached the fountain in the middle of the park and sat down, enjoying the sun on our faces as we ate our melting ice cream.

"That will be the day," I mocked. "Pretty Princess Paxton in a relationship? Give me a break."

"I haven't heard you call him that since we were twelve."

The name had literally come to be because of his ridiculously pretty eyes. That was the extent of my creativity as a child when it came to nicknames. That and Piss Your Pants Paxton, which I regretted since the day I vomited that one out. Poor guy had spilled a drink, and I made everyone believe something different.

Carla continued, "Ever think it's about time to stop picking on him?"

"I haven't picked on him in years. It would be simple to

continue, though, because he's such an easy target."

"What do you mean?"

"He was mowing the lawn for my mom the other day and was as silent and moody as he was back in school."

"Really?"

I cocked my head to the side. "Does that surprise you?"

"It's just—" Her eyes grew wide. "Speak of the devil..."

I followed her line of sight and saw him walking along like he didn't have a care in the world. To my displeasure, Carla waved him over. "Hey, Pax. Over here."

He looked to Carla and nodded. When his eyes moved to me, his shoulders sagged. I could almost see him calculating whether he could get away with a quick escape and evade or if he was stuck.

He moved hesitantly before shifting in our direction. His eyes were focused on Carla while he completely ignored me. I had to pinch myself to make sure I was there. As he neared, he did more than smile at Carla; he lit up like high beams on a dark highway.

His was a massive, dazzling grin that made my heart beat faster, and my insides turn to pudding.

"Hey, future big sister. Getting your sugar fix for the day?"

"You bet. What are you doing by yourself on the weekend? You haven't been roped into helping anyone today, have you?"

He shook his head. "No, today is a free day. Figured I'd take in the weather and appreciate your brother having plans. Ever since you and Owen got together, he's become my twin. Follows me everywhere like an orphaned puppy."

"He's used to having me around. I'm sure he's lonely. Thanks for filling in for me."

The two of them continued talking easily, as I watched in disbelief. I'd never heard Paxton speak so much. Hadn't heard him say more than a sentence at a time since I'd known him. His voice was deep and low and hot as hell. That voice was a superpower that could make a girl swoon.

Who was this guy? I hadn't met this Paxton, only the silent brooding one he let me see.

"By the way, Pax," Carla began, "has Owen given you the updated stage design?"

He scrubbed his face with his palms. "You're kidding, right? What did I tell him?"

"Aww, I'm sorry, but I think the new design might actually be easier to build."

"Sure, it will."

"You don't sound convinced."

For a moment, it looked as if he was going to say something, but then he moved forward, bent down, and licked my ice cream.

"It was melting," he said simply, flicking his tongue against his upper lip to remove some residual pink cream before turning back to Carla. The action left me stunned and speechless, which was a rarity for me.

I shook my head and tried to clear it. What the hell was going on? I'd entered an alternate universe where Paxton Cooper was no longer a tall lanky mute, but a sexy ice cream thief with a whiskey-smooth voice and a body carved from stone.

"Pax, we're doing drinks next Saturday in that new place that's opening," Carla said. "Make sure you don't get roped into helping someone out that afternoon so you can join us."

His upper lip twitched. "What's wrong with Reilly's?"

"Frazier Falls is getting a new place?" I asked. "I thought it would forever be Reilly's or Huck's."

Paxton frowned at the mention of Huck's.

Carla threw her hands in the air. "Hallelujah, we were all surprised. Either way, I have the place reserved on Saturday.

It's lucky you chose to come home early because now you can join us at the Bobbly Olive."

I smiled, glancing at Paxton out of the corner of my eye. His expression was, once more, unreadable. "I look forward to it."

He glanced at his cell. "I better be off."

"I thought you had a free day?" I asked.

He stared at me. His damn blue eyes looked so hard at me I swore I'd ignite.

"I do. Nothing to do and no one I feel obligated to see."

Carla whipped her head between Paxton and me, then burst out laughing. "Okay, fair enough. Have fun."

He kissed Carla on the cheek before he left, deliberately not looking at me before walking away.

I turned toward her. "Who the hell is that because it sure wasn't the Paxton I knew."

"Oh, Rosie, you poor, poor girl."

"What do you mean by that?"

"I think you'll find that he has long since surpassed Owen as the hottie of Frazier Falls. Everyone loves him—not least because he's happy to help with menial tasks, but the women find his charm irresistible."

"Charm? And now he speaks?"

"Is that so much of a surprise?"

"A freaking mind blower."

"He still speaks way less than anyone else I've ever known, but that also means he never says something he doesn't mean. It's worth listening when he actually chooses to talk."

"He seemed damn chatty with you."

"Yeah, you're right," she said, a little surprised. "He speaks to me much more now that I'm part of the family, but even taking that into consideration, he spoke quite a lot before I entered the picture. I wonder—"

47

"Ugh, I don't want to know." I was sure I knew what she was going to say was maybe he thought I wasn't worth talking to.

A cold trickle of ice cream ran over my hand to remind me I hadn't finished my cone, but looking at it only recapped that Paxton had chosen to lick it. Did I dare lick over the spot where he had? Wouldn't that be admitting that somewhere deep inside, I wanted to experience his lips and tongue? Confusion at my mixed feelings twisted my insides. When I moved past the trash can, I tossed the cone inside.

Carla pouted. "I'd have eaten that."

"I refuse to be responsible if you don't fit into your wedding dress."

"That's a risk I was willing to take."

A giggle graduated to a laugh. "One day, your metabolism will slow, and I swear, you'll regret every double scoop you ever devoured."

"We all have our guilty pleasures. Yours was teasing Pax. Do you regret that?"

I scowled. "You're not funny."

"Not trying to be."

I looked down the path in the direction he'd walked. He was gone, but he'd left me with feelings I wasn't ready to confront.

Guilt.

Remorse.

Agitation.

Anger.

Attraction.

Arousal.

The way he treated me set up an interesting precedent for the next three weeks. It was in that moment I promised myself one thing. He was going to talk to me, even if I had to tie him up and torture the words out of him.

CHAPTER SEVEN

PAXTON

I couldn't believe I hadn't left the park after saying goodbye to Carla. Even worse, I was hiding in order to watch Rose.

It was bad enough to hide in the first place, but to watch her like a creepy stalker? I couldn't believe what I was doing, but for some reason, I couldn't stop.

"Why did I eat her stupid ice cream? Fool…" I muttered, resulting in curious glances from a group of local kids. I placed a finger to my lips to let them know to stay quiet about my presence. They grinned in return, clearly thinking they were now involved in my secretive game.

I didn't know what I was looking for. I was simply … looking.

My original plan of giving her the classic silent treatment had been cut short because of Carla. She'd have blown it if I tried that in front of her, so I figured it would be better to go straight into the second part of the plan. Make sure Rose knew I was deliberately ignoring her, which seemed to infuriate her. A promising first result.

Taking all of that into consideration, I knew I should

leave the park. There was no doubt I would run into her again, and I'd have an opportunity to annoy her.

Thinking about that made me pause. My plan to ignore Rose had been my way of dealing with her close proximity. The more time I could spend away from that woman, the better. So why was I looking forward to the next time I could be near her? Why was I still in the damn park?

Disgusted with myself, I stared at the path and saw both Carla and Rose had gone. Carla headed out of the park in the direction of Owen's house. I wasn't sure where Rose had gone and spun around to see if somehow, she'd found me. The public areas were Rose free.

This was ridiculous. I crept out of my hiding place as subtly as possible and headed toward home but remembered I needed groceries since no home-cooked meal was coming my way today.

Groaning because I'd have to cook, I headed in the direction of Wilkes', my mood gloomier than it had been when I'd entered the park. My brothers gave me a hard time about my volunteer work, but I rarely had a day where I didn't have a meal.

The streets were quiet for a Saturday. Everyone was most likely by the creek, or in their back yards since they weren't in the park. That was perfect for me. It meant I could enjoy the sunshine without being disturbed.

As soon as I had that thought, a woman appeared at the crossroads ahead of me and turned onto the same street, going in the same direction.

"You've got to be kidding me." The words shot out of my mouth too loudly when I realized who it was. Rose stopped in her tracks, the faint breeze softly billowing the delicate fabric of her dress around her legs. She turned to face me.

Instinct told me to walk back the way I came, but stubbornness moved me forward. Shoving my hands in my pockets, I pressed on, as if I didn't care she was there at all.

She raised an eyebrow as I got closer. "Are you following me?"

I wrestled with the idea of not responding. When I reached her, I sauntered past and said, "Nope."

Despite walking away quickly, she rushed to catch up.

"Why the hell were you behind me when you supposedly left the park ages ago?"

"I'm on a walk."

Clearly, she still wasn't getting the message from my brisk pace and short, clipped sentences. She continued to walk by my side, though it was obvious I wanted to be alone.

"Seems like a pretty circuitous walk if you only ended up two minutes outside of the park after walking for fifteen."

I didn't reply. What could I say? I'd been watching her. I'd have laughed if it wasn't for her walking beside me, watching me intently with a frown pulling down the corners of her plump pink lips.

"Now you're back to not speaking? Geez, Paxton. I don't get you."

Her nose twitched in frustration when I continued to ignore her. My pace slowed. No use tiring myself out when she did all she could to keep up with me. Maybe she'd get bored if I walked at a snail's pace, and she would move ahead of me.

This seemed to confuse her more, which was somewhat satisfying given that she'd confused me my entire life.

"What are you doing?" she asked. "What's the point of all this?" She waved her hand about like a human flyswatter.

I spared her a glance. "What do you mean?"

"You know what I mean." She fisted her hips and stomped her foot then had to double step to catch up.

"Then you know what I mean."

She looked ready to tear her hair from her head. "Paxton, you're an adult. Why don't you act like one?"

"Not speaking to you isn't juvenile behavior, it's self-preservation."

It took me a few steps before I realized she had stopped. I resisted the urge to turn around, instead choosing to continue on toward Wilkes'.

"Princess Paxton."

I froze before spinning around to face her.

"What did you call me?" My voice was loud enough for her and the next county to hear.

"I called you princess," she shouted back. "At least that got a reaction out of you."

I marched over and pinned her against the closest parked car without thinking, my mind blind with years of suppressed rage. Her eyes went wide with alarm.

"Say that again to my face."

"I … Jeez, Paxton, it was a joke." Her voice shook.

I could tell by the expression on her face she knew she'd taken things too far. I tightened my grip on her shoulders, watching her, looking for something, but like in the park, I had no idea what it was I needed to see.

"Paxton?"

"You're not sorry. You never were."

Her saucer-like eyes stayed on me. "How would you know?"

I let go of her and turned away to continue my walk down the street. After a few moments, she appeared at my side once more.

"What the hell is going on?"

"Leave me alone."

"Paxton …"

"Stop saying my name as if we're friends." My hands ached from clenching them into fists.

"I can think of a few other options."

The tense muscles of my jaw twitched. "I bet. You were always good at name games."

"You were always good at being an asshole."

I glanced at her, scowling. "Whatever. Go bother someone else."

"I'm going to Wilkes'."

"Choose another route."

"We're two minutes away from the damn place. I'm pressing forward."

"Fine."

I made an abrupt right turn and veered onto another street. Going to the store could wait. Getting away from Rose could not.

With her hands on her hips, she yelled, "Are you seriously doing this because you can't deal with me for two minutes?"

"I don't see a problem. Have a pleasant afternoon."

For a few seconds, I was certain she'd follow me, but her absence made it apparent she wouldn't. A sigh of relief left my body, but my gut was twisting and turning.

So much for keeping my cool and gaining the upper hand. I haven't been that openly angry in … forever.

That reality shook me. Only she could have ever elicited that much fury. Not even Brady Huck, whom I hated, could do this to me. Maybe it was because I hadn't seen her in fourteen years or maybe it was something else.

It was only when I reached my house that I remembered I had no food. After roaring in frustration, I picked up my phone and called Rich. I would have called Eli, but lately, he'd been occupied by a certain Irish redhead. I couldn't find fault with that. At least he was happy. That left me with Rich; we were both odd men out. What a pair.

He picked up immediately.

"Hi Pax, I just got in. What's up?"

"Why don't you come over for dinner? You'll have to bring food."

Rich laughed. "You missed me?"

"No. I'm hungry."

"Do you have beer?"

"It's the one thing I do have in the fridge."

"I'll be over within the hour."

I hung up, feeling more in control of my emotions. Rich would know something was wrong, but he wouldn't push me to talk about it. We weren't at a place in our friendship to share secrets. I needed someone who wouldn't push and prod and twist me until I completely lost it.

Someone, unlike Rose.

Next time I saw her, I promised I wouldn't let her get to me. If I reacted, she'd win.

Groaning, I opened my refrigerator to get a beer, screwing off the lid and gulping down half of the contents in seconds.

At least for tonight, I could drink and forget. Who in the hell was I kidding? Rose wasn't someone I was likely ever to forget.

CHAPTER EIGHT

ROSE

When I saw Nick calling, I let out a noise of delight. Grabbing my phone, I rushed to answer.

"You have no idea how good it is to hear your voice." I collapsed onto my bed, the soft comforter hugging my bottom.

He chuckled. "If you were going to miss me that fast, you shouldn't have been so quick to run away from New York."

"You wouldn't have reacted the exact same way if you found out your boyfriend was cheating on you and didn't give a damn?"

"No, because I've never been in a position for that to happen. The scenario would require me to have a long-term boyfriend in the first place."

"Trust me; you don't want one. Men suck."

"You sound like a woman scorned. Remind me not to get on your bad side."

"Me—a bad side? I don't know what you're talking about."

Nick sighed as I fell to my back on my bed. The sun had set, and it had grown cooler after the unseasonably hot day. My entire body felt like it had been scorched, but that was due to Paxton. He'd seared me with his words. Words said in anger that held many truths. I hated that he had the ability to flay me open.

"You definitely have a bad side," Nick said. "I don't think you realize how many people are scared of you, including me."

Am I that rotten? "What do you mean?"

"The casual almost-offensive nicknames, the quips, the pointed comments—"

"They're not—people don't think I actually mean any of that, do they?" How could anyone take my words seriously? Sure, I dished out a lot, but I wasn't the only one. "Everyone talks to each other like that. I don't say stuff because I don't like someone. I've flung snarky comments at you as much as anyone else."

"Your comments are on a whole other level than everyone else. Your words strike at the jugular. I bet you were a skilled bully in high school."

"I was not. Teasing isn't bullying—"

"You were a mean girl, weren't you? I'm so disappointed in you."

"No, I—"

But then I paused. While I'd always considered my teasing of Paxton to be standard small-town name-calling and the like—never mind that I stopped once we reached high school — his actions earlier today suggested the way I'd treated him had affected him far worse than I'd known.

Our parents had been close friends. The entire Cooper family had been at my parents' wedding. It was natural that they had tried to push him and me to be friends. While his older brothers were busy charming everyone around them, I was left with a sulking, silent boy who stood there as I called him names. I wasn't the only one who picked on him. What Brady Huck put him through in high school was what anyone would consider horrific bullying. If he was affected by anything, it should have been that. Brady had been so bad that even I'd felt sorry for Paxton. I'd even considered helping him out.

Why was it me that he hated so bad? Had I taken things so far without knowing it? How could I have known it if he never said anything?

God, the guy frustrated me, and he didn't even do anything.

"Rose? You still there?" A hint of concern colored Nick's voice.

"Yeah, sorry. I think I was having a bit of a life crisis."

"Don't take what I said to heart. I was only making fun of you. You know everyone loves you despite you."

"There's definitely someone from my past who doesn't feel the same."

"Did you break his heart, or did you like him, and he didn't like you back? Is that why you bullied him?"

My mouth hung open. "Who even said it was a guy?"

"Your immediate reaction confirms it. Was it the former or the latter?"

"Yuck, I did not like Paxton." Just the thought of liking him made my insides twist and to be accused of anything but loathing him, made my throat burn.

"Did you break his heart?"

"Trust me, he did not like me when he was a boy, and he likes me less as a man."

"Now we're talking." It sounded as if Nick slapped his hands together. I could see him in my mind rubbing them like he was plotting a world takeover. "Sounds like you're having a fun reunion back home. Is he hot? I want details."

I closed my eyes and pictured Paxton shirtless in my mom's yard. Hot didn't begin to describe him. He was drop-dead gorgeous. "Why does it matter?"

"It always matters. Did you say his name was Paxton?"

"Yes, Paxton Cooper," I finished, then immediately regretted it. "Nick, don't you dare—"

"Too late. I've found him. Damn, this guy is beyond attractive. What was going through your head when you picked on him?"

"He obviously didn't look like that when we were in school together." I reached for my computer and pulled up Paxton's social media profile. My fingertips traced his handsome face. "Typical ugly duckling story. He got hot after high school."

"Uh-huh." Nick didn't sound convinced. "Someone this hot is never not attractive, even when they're going through their awkward years. Maybe you didn't notice. Maybe you were blind."

It was an interesting point of view. In high school, Paxton had Eli beside him—a handsome human being who demanded attention. Surely it wasn't all that surprising that nobody thought Paxton was attractive by comparison?

In truth, even though he hadn't filled out his tall frame, there was nothing that made him unattractive. Rather, it had been the way he carried himself. He had been awkward, reserved, and introverted. His shoulders were always hunched. His head was kept down. His eyes were permanently glued to the floor.

Those eyes. Big beautiful lakes of blue.

"Fine, Nick, he wasn't unattractive even then," I admitted, which felt close to having my teeth pulled out. "Awkward and lanky but not … ugly." Why was it so hard to admit the truth? He had always been handsome.

Nick burst out laughing. "You're so transparent. How did you get to your thirties lying to yourself about all this stuff?"

"Very easily, thank you. I excel at self-deceit. And whether

DEFEND ME

the guy was always hot or not doesn't change anything about the rest of him."

"I guess I'll never be able to confirm with my own eyes and ears."

"Oh, but you could, actually …" My voice trailed off when I suddenly remembered I had an open plus-one to Carla's wedding. "Want to be my date for my friend's wedding?"

"That's like asking me if I want alcohol. Obviously, it's a yes. Will I get to meet this guy?"

"Unfortunately, yes."

"Ooh," he cooed. "The day keeps getting better and better."

"The new issue of Flair comes out a week before the wedding. You can probably wrangle a few extra days off to join me here if you want. I mean, it's still Frazier Falls."

"I'll take any break I can get," Nick chuckled. "I'll get the days approved. I don't suppose this guy has any equally attractive, not-quite-so-straight brothers who'll be at the wedding?"

"Well, it's actually his eldest brother who's getting married, so that rules him out, and Eli also has a girlfriend and is as straight as a ruler."

"Are they all beautiful?" Nick asked, sounding disappointed.

"It's the Cooper curse. Beauty wasted on a man or three. Oh, but—"

"Yes?" His tone pitched up.

"No … never mind," I murmured, thinking of what my mom had said about Rich Stevenson. That had been groundless conjecture that I should ask Carla about. "I'll get back to you about the potential dating material at the wedding."

"Don't get my hopes up for nothing," he joked.

"I would never."

"Speaking of disappointing men, I actually called you for a reason."

"What, you didn't want to talk to me for the sheer thrill of it?"

"Well, that was a given. But trust me, you'll want to hear this."

I shoved my computer aside, giving Paxton's picture one more glance and moved off my bed to the seat underneath my open window. "Fire away, then."

"You'll never guess who's come into the office the last three days asking for you."

"I don't like where this is going."

"Guess."

I massaged my temples with my fingers, already feeling a headache coming on at the mere thought of it. "Please tell me it wasn't James scum-bag Rivers."

"One and the same."

"Why did he come three days in a row? Didn't you tell him to piss off?"

"It was Sadie who dealt with him on the first day," Nick explained, "and of course, she had no clue what happened between the two of you. She didn't even know you'd gone on vacation. The second day I dealt with him, but I didn't want to say where you were in case he tried to contact you."

"I blocked his number, his ability to contact me on social media and email. He won't be able to get in touch."

"That explains why he came back on the third day. Obviously, he knows you have Carla's wedding coming up, so he asked me if you'd gone home. I told him it didn't matter where you were because you made it clear you didn't want to see him."

"And what did he say?"

"He said he made a mistake and that he's sorry. Can you believe it? Says he was too drunk and what happened the night at the bar would never happen again. Asked me to pass along the message in the hopes you'd forgive him."

"The son of a bitch," I exclaimed. "Who does he think he is? I spent all year fawning over him and he—"

"Honey, I know," Nick cut in, his tone placating. "I told him if he wanted to pass on a message like that, he could do it himself. Then I had him escorted out of the building."

I went from angry to ecstatic in a flash. "Oh my—oh my God, did you do that? You had him kicked out?"

"You bet your ass I did. No one gets to mess with my mean girl but me."

"Nick, you're the best, you know that?" I said between bouts of laughter. "Thanks for calling me. I needed to hear that."

"I thought you might. It's easier to get over someone when you know how worthless they are. You made a lucky escape. And hey, now you can make up with this Paxton guy."

I hung up the phone on reflex. Nick called me back immediately.

"Rude," he muttered.

"You deserved it. Stop talking nonsense."

"He can't be worse than James, and at least he's cuter."

"Hardly a benchmark I'd use." I stared out at the last of the orange creamsicle sun sinking into the horizon.

"True. Anyway. I have a bottle of wine and a crappy nineties film with my name on it. I love you, and I'll see you in a few days."

"Love you too, Nick."

"Night."

After I hung up the phone, I collapsed back onto my bed. Nick had given me a lot to think about—most of which I didn't want floating around in my head in the first place.

It was all about Paxton. Why had my long-awaited return home become about him?

I thought of him slamming me against the car earlier that afternoon. I gathered that the action was supposed to have scared me, and it had, but not in the way he had probably wanted.

It had scared me because it made me realize how passionate the guy was, and I had missed that facet of him until now. That made the whole pinning me against a car thing…

I suppressed a shudder.

Kind of hot.

CHAPTER NINE

PAXTON

For me, the quiet guy, to come back to my high school campus meant I had drastically regressed as a person. Sitting behind the bleachers, resting my head against the wire fencing, and smoking a cigarette wasn't my normal go-to. Last time I'd smoked had been my junior year of high school. It was the only year of my life I'd picked up the nasty habit. To this day, I had no clue why I'd done it and had no reason why I wanted to smoke now.

Thinking about how ridiculous it was, I looked at the cigarette in disgust before throwing it to the ground and crushing it with my heel as I sighed out a final puff of acrid smoke.

With Carla and Owen's wedding only two weeks away, Frazier Falls was coming to life, and all the former residents were crawling out of the woodwork. It felt unnerving running into people I hadn't seen in years and not knowing what to say, or if I wanted to engage at all. Despite that, I forced myself through the motions of polite conversation with everyone who had recognized me. As one of Owen's brothers and groomsmen, it was part of the gig.

Why couldn't they show up on the day of and leave town the next? I liked the way Frazier Falls was normally. I didn't need ghosts of my past, haunting the streets and bothering my every waking moment.

The sound of crunching gravel to my left caught my attention. I turned to see who had found me, then immediately grumbled.

"Why are you here?" I shifted my body away from Rose. I was half inclined to leave altogether, but I didn't see why I should be the one to go. I had been here first.

Rose stopped a few feet away from me.

"I wasn't aware I was forbidden to take a walk down memory lane."

I let out a bitter laugh. "When were you ever behind the bleachers?"

"You and I both know you're not too stupid or innocent to realize that everyone used the back of the bleachers for something or another."

I didn't respond. I wanted nothing more than for her to get the message and leave of her own volition. Minutes passed, and she didn't move an inch.

I turned to glower at her. "There's a lot of bleacher left. Do you have to be right here?"

She seemed to hesitate for a moment then let out a resolute "Yes" as she sat herself right down next to me.

I stood up to leave, but she grabbed my wrist.

"What?" I asked, pulling away in the process.

Her expression was unreadable. I had no idea what she was thinking. "Stay for a minute, Paxton," she said. "I need to … apologize … for a lot of things."

I quirked a brow. "You followed me here to do that?"

She shook her head, eyes slightly wide. "No. This was an accidental meeting. I didn't come here to apologize, but … to be honest."

"Sounds like you're unbelievably sorry." I sounded angry. I couldn't believe I was upset. Rose Rogers wasn't important to me.

"Paxton—"

"Fine," I interrupted as I turned to face her and settled back with the fence pressing into my skin. "You have five minutes. Which is four more than you deserve."

She glanced at me out of the corner of her eye. "Thank you," she said quietly.

I looked away, staring out at the football field before us. So much had happened on that grass. Lots of memories of playing ball with my dad and brothers. Other memories not so nice. "Go on then."

She didn't say anything. Instead, she sniffed the air a few times then looked around before eyeing the ground below us. "Were you smoking?"

"Yep, so what?"

"I didn't think you were the smoking type."

"I'm not."

"So why—"

I stared at her, silently pushing for her to stop changing the subject.

She released an exasperated breath. "I'm sorry for pushing your buttons the other day. It was immature of me."

"And?"

She stared up at the starlit sky above us with a look on her face that suggested she'd rather yank her teeth out than continue speaking. "And it may have recently come to my attention the way I treated you when we were younger was bordering on unacceptable."

I nearly choked. "Bordering on it?"

"Ugh, fine! It was completely out of line, and I should never have acted that way toward you when you'd done nothing wrong. There! Are you happy?"

"Marginally."

She fisted her hands and tucked them tightly to her sides. "There's no pleasing you, is there?"

"You think a pained ten-second apology is equivalent to the years of bullshit I had to put up with from you?"

Rose, like her name, wilted in front of me. Her shoulders fell forward, and her expression softened.

"No, but it's better for me to start owning up to my mistakes now rather than never, right?"

I didn't reply. Both of us knew the answer to her question. Never in all my days did I consider I'd hear any type of I'm sorry from her, so this was a banner moment.

I spared a glance in her direction. "Would you have apologized to me if I hadn't lashed out the other day?"

"Don't make me answer that."

"That answered it for me, so no need."

"Paxton—"

"You use my name a lot. Why?"

"That's because … because I never called you by your name before." She seemed to realize the reality of what she was saying as she was saying it, which was interesting to watch. "I guess that's weird, huh? I only ever called you by your name if I put princess or something else in front of it."

I wrinkled my nose in disgust. "Don't go there."

She laughed. "It's not as if I called you that after middle school, though."

"Not to my face, you didn't."

She moved her hand like she was slicing the air with a sword. "Touché."

"I can't believe it took you until high school to find something better to do than bother me," I ended up saying. "Still can't believe you ended up as a cheerleader."

"You say that like it's a bad thing."

"You only did it because you liked the way people looked at you when you wore the uniform."

She looked surprised. "How do you—why would you say that?"

I studied her. "Because I didn't like you doesn't mean I didn't know you. You're a fairly transparent person. What other people think is what's most important."

"Yes, but ... when did you even find the time to get to know me?"

"Funnily enough, if you stop talking long enough to actually listen to people, you can learn a lot. And if you don't spend any time talking whatsoever—"

"Then I guess you can learn a lot about lots of people," she finished, letting out a whoosh of air between her teeth as she rolled the sleeves of her hoodie up. "Why is it still so warm out? It's nearly midnight, and I'm too warm in a hoodie and shorts."

"I don't think I've ever seen you in a sweatshirt that was actually yours."

She looked at me quizzically. "What's that supposed to mean?"

"It means exactly what it means. You would always steal your boyfriend's. There was Liam Potts, and Reggie Wyatt, and—"

"Oh my God, why do you remember all of this?" Her face grew redder and redder under the glow of the moon as she covered her eyes with her hands. "This is mortifying."

"Sometimes I wondered if you dated them simply to get the hoodies," I said quietly. "Because you knew they looked good on you. All oversized and not matching the rest of your perfectly constructed outfit. It was a clever way to appear endearing to everyone while putting zero effort in and getting the attention you needed."

"You're not very nice," she said, though she didn't look

upset—merely embarrassed. "It was a good thing you never spoke in school; otherwise, you'd have ripped people to shreds."

"I had Eli as an older brother. Is it any wonder I learned how to insult?"

Another heavy sigh left her lungs. "I guess not. But, hey, if you'd have been talkative, you'd have been one hell of a popular guy. So why didn't you talk?"

I looked down at my shoes for a few moments, not sure if I wanted to explain myself. Eventually, I said, "That's the way I was. They initially told my parents I was high functioning on the autism scale."

"Oh." Her voice lowered. "I didn't know."

"It wasn't true."

"There was a different reason?"

"I was bored. I'm off the charts smart, and child's play wasn't my thing." I looked up at the stars trying to make out the different constellations and focused on Cassiopeia. "However, emotionally, I was a child with an adult brain. By the time I realized sitting back and analyzing my world was viewed as odd, I didn't know how to go about fixing the problem. I thought the teasing would get worse if suddenly I started talking. I kept quiet and hoped people would leave me alone until I could start fresh at college, where my intellect could speak for itself."

I looked up abruptly. She had moved up close enough for me to feel her body heat. "Since you shared that, I'll share this."

I frowned. "What?" Was she going to tell me she had a Mensa score for her IQ too?

"Starting fresh in college. I was dying to get out of here and work out who I was ... or who I wanted to be."

"I think everyone wanted the same thing."

She paused for a moment to take that in, then asked, "If

you wanted to start fresh, then why did you come back to Frazier Falls once you graduated?"

"I realized how much I loved the place when I was away from it. Once everyone around me had grown up, I didn't have to deal with any of the nonsense from school. Owen and Eli had set up Cooper Construction, which I wanted to be a part of, so I had lots of reasons for wanting to come back."

"I'm happy for you, Paxton. I am."

I glanced at her. Her lips were curled into a genuine smile that lit up her eyes. There was a light breeze on the air, gently twisting and turning her hair about her face. In any other circumstance, I'd be cursing myself for thinking about how beautiful she was, but not tonight.

I resisted the urge to tuck away the few strands waving about in front of her face. "What's it like for you being back in Frazier Falls after so long of a hiatus? Your mom told me you work as a fashion editor in New York."

She literally beamed. If I thought she was attractive before...

"I work for a magazine called Flair. I love it, but it's a high-stress job, and I haven't had an opportunity to take a vacation in years. I guess there's never a right time to take off when you work for a magazine like that. It's good to be home for longer than a couple of days. God knows my mom is loving having me back. Although..."

"Although?"

She blushed furiously as she looked away from me. "She keeps trying to insist the two of us go on a date."

I let out a bark of laughter. "Be lucky this is the first time she's ever said such things to you. I've been hearing it from her for years now."

"No way. You never declined? Or, I don't know... told her you hated me?"

"I always changed the subject. Seemed a little callous to tell her I wasn't a fan of her one and only child."

She laughed. "I guess I should thank you on her behalf. That's nice of you not to ruin her epic fantasy of seeing the two of us together."

"I think she wants me as her son-in-law so she can guiltlessly have me help her with everything until the end of time."

"I wouldn't put it past her."

We laughed a little at that before settling into a comfortable silence.

I didn't want to admit I was having a good time with Rose, and yet, here I was, having fun like it was the most natural thing in the world.

Some part of me knew such feelings spelled disaster for me, but for now, I didn't care.

CHAPTER TEN

ROSE

It was something out of an alternate universe to be sitting behind my high school bleachers, talking to Paxton as if we'd been the best of friends for years. Or at least friends who hadn't seen each other in a lifetime. Maybe even friends who had grown apart and were now reconnecting.

But he and I both knew we had never been friends. Not back then. In all honesty, even though he was speaking to me, I couldn't see how we could be friends now. Despite all of that, I was having a good time talking to the man he'd become. More than a good time, if I was being honest. I hadn't been this comfortable talking to anyone since I first met Nick. Not once had I been able to speak with James this easily. Not during the entire time we dated. There was always a disconnect. Was it because of me or him? More than once, Paxton insinuated I was less than authentic, and I knew he was right. I'd adopted the personality of every girl I wanted to be, hoping that, along the way, I'd find myself. I never had. I hid behind Prada bags and high-end cosmetics. Labels and brands that said more about me than my own personality could.

And yet, here I was, laughing and joking with a man who'd spent most of his life knowing exactly who I was and justifiably hating everything about me.

"You said you like it here now that everyone has grown up," I said after a minute of silence. "Is that true of everyone?"

He eyed me warily. "I take it this question is about one person in particular?"

I nodded. "Brady Huck."

Paxton failed to suppress a shiver; his expression twisted into something similar to disgust. I didn't like seeing his handsome face marred by displeasure. I risked placing a hand on his arm, my fingers touching his skin below the hem of his T-shirt sleeve. Even though it wasn't the time or place or person for such a reaction, my heartbeat thumped wildly inside my chest.

"You don't have to answer the question," I ended up saying, suddenly feeling nervous. "It was a crappy question."

He glanced down at my hand on his arm but didn't move away from it. He lifted his eyes to look at me. Under the light of the moon, the deep blue of his irises appeared almost purple.

"It's fine," he murmured. "I avoid him. Eli and Owen sometimes go to Huck's for a drink, but I never join. I have no idea if he's grown up at all and in all actuality, I don't care."

"Owen and Eli don't know?"

He laughed somewhat bitterly. "Eli knows some. Given his predisposition for collecting gossip, I'd be surprised if he didn't know everything that happened in Frazier Falls."

I smiled. "He would definitely have an opinion if he did."

"It's precisely why I don't bring it up. What would be the purpose of saying anything? It's not as if telling them would change what happened. The past should be left in the past."

"It sure would be gratifying to watch all three of you take revenge against Brady."

His eyes widened. "You don't like him?"

"No. You sound surprised."

"He was always hanging around you. I just assumed."

I grimaced. "He may have hung around me, but I didn't hang around him. I didn't like what he did to you."

"You didn't like what *he* did to me?"

"There's a difference between childhood name-calling and what he did. And yet, you seem far more pissed at me. Why is that?"

He looked away. "I don't know. Maybe …"

"Maybe what?"

He sighed. "Maybe I expected more from you."

I hadn't expected him to say that. The words stung, biting into my heart like an angry army of red ants.

He stood up suddenly, making me jump in surprise. His eyes stayed fixed on me as he offered a hand to help me up.

"It's about time the two of us got home." His expression held no negative emotions. His eyes were as clear and beautiful as they had been earlier—as they had always been.

"My mom is probably waiting up for me, even though I told her not to." I dusted off my shorts as we walked away from the high school campus.

He chuckled softly. "She'll still be drinking wine, knowing her."

"I wouldn't be surprised in the slightest if she was."

Paxton knew my mother well. How was it that he could have become as familiar as family?

When we neared the creek, I expected him to say his goodbye, but he continued walking along the water's edge beside me.

"Are you walking me home?" It somewhat thrilled me that he'd make sure I got home safely.

"In a roundabout way. I live about ten minutes farther up the creek than your mom."

I hadn't even considered where he might live. Somehow everyone had stayed the same in my mind. "It was a bit stupid of me to think you still lived in your parents' house." It was a foolish thought.

"We sold it. None of us wanted to, but it deserved a family."

"You all live alone?"

He glanced at me; his eyebrows knitted together in thought. "Have you seen us? We need our own places. Putting us together is like housing a dog, a cat, and a mouse and hoping everyone lives." He stopped abruptly, which caught me off guard.

"I imagine it would be tough living a lifetime with your siblings."

He shook his head. "It was tough living with them for as long as I did."

"Are you okay?" There was something quiet and contemplative about him. Not the silent Paxton I thought I knew but the thinking man I was getting acquainted with.

"I'm fine," he replied as we continued walking. "Just reflecting on all that we said tonight."

"We should have spoken sooner." It was like a lifetime had passed in hours. So many hurts addressed and no solutions; only a half-assed apology that should have been more. Was it possible that was all he needed to heal his wounds?

"I didn't realize being a fashion editor lent itself to such deep and meaningful discussions."

"Very funny." I rolled my eyes. "I was the top of my class in English at high school and college. Would it come as much of a surprise if there was a poet hidden somewhere deep inside me?"

"Deep, deep, deep inside, hiding behind snarky nicknames and immature taunts, maybe." His lips curled into a faint smile.

"That's ... fair." I realized there was no way I could argue the point. Not with him having been on the receiving end of my worst me.

He hummed tunelessly as we walked along the grassy bank by the creek.

"You're in a good mood," I pointed out.

"And?"

"And I don't think I've ever seen you in a good mood. Not when you're around me."

"Very funny."

Paxton grasped onto the sleeve of my hoodie and turned me around unexpectedly, which set my heart hammering. "What are you doing?"

He pointed over to the other side of the creek. "This is where Owen and Carla want me to build their floating wedding stage. From all the way over there to where we're standing."

"That seems ... grandiose." I peered into the darkness to try and gauge how big the resulting platform would be.

"I know, right!?" he exclaimed, enthusiastic in his indignation. "They want it to be large enough to use as the dance floor for the reception as well as the location of the ceremony. I'm dreading having to build it."

"I guess they wouldn't ask you to do it if they didn't believe you weren't the best person for the job. I'd call that a compliment."

"Yeah, I know. Doesn't make the job any easier, though."

"Something tells me you won't have a problem building it, Mr. Mensa." I looked at him in the moonlight, taking in his tightly muscled arms, the bulk of his shoulders, and the abs I knew were hidden beneath his T-shirt.

A lock of his hair had fallen across his forehead, and I resisted the urge to reach up and sweep it to the side.

Damn, he looked good, I thought wistfully. Who would have thought?

He watched me watching him. His eyes lifted. "Are you checking me out?"

Even in the darkness, I knew he could see my face flushing scarlet. I didn't have to see it to feel the heat that rose to my cheeks. "No. I'm not."

He laughed. "You are. You're not even being subtle about it. Do I look that different from high school?"

"Yes and no."

"That seems contradictory."

"Exactly. It's confusing. You don't slouch or keep your head down anymore, and you've finally grown into your height, but ... you're still the same, I guess."

"You guess?"

"Look, as hard as it is for me to admit, you were always cute."

I looked up at him, expecting him to reply. Instead, he glanced behind me at the creek. I knew what he was going to do a split second before he did it. He reached forward and pushed me.

The water bit into my skin like stinging frozen bees, a stark and shocking difference from the uncharacteristically warm May air. When I broke the surface, his laughter filled the air.

"I h-hope you're h-happy now," I stammered, teeth chattering from the cold.

He reached down to help me out of the water. "You know you deserved that."

"Y-you're lucky I d-didn't pull you in w-with me."

That only made him laugh harder. "As if you could pull me in. Come on. Your house is up ahead. Best not to make too much noise so you can run up to your room and get changed without your mom asking questions."

"I'm sure she'd love to h-hear about how you threw me into the c-creek at midnight."

"I'm sure she would."

When we reached my back yard, he stopped with me for a moment. "Thank you for apologizing." His voice was quiet and sincere.

"I—thanks for letting me apologize." What else could I say?

His gaze was locked on my face, his eyes searching for … something. My blood raced through my veins, its rapid path leading to dizziness.

For a moment, it almost seemed like he would kiss me. And I think I almost wanted it to happen. But seconds passed, and he shook his head.

"This was a bizarre night. Make sure to keep warm when you get inside, so you don't catch a cold."

"I'm blaming you if I do."

"Completely fair."

"Okay … night, Paxton," I said, a little awkwardly. It felt like we were supposed to hug or—I didn't know—shake hands or something. Something to put a solid end to the evening.

Instead, I gave him a final smile and walked through my back yard, opening and closing the kitchen door as silently as possible.

The house was dark. If my mom was still awake, she had retired to her bedroom.

When I looked through the window, Paxton was gone. It was as if he had never been there in the first place.

CHAPTER ELEVEN

PAXTON

Carla and Owen's cocktail party was upon me before I remembered to make an excuse to miss it. I supposed Carla had attached Owen's name to the party to ensure I went, so no excuse would work.

Under ordinary circumstances, I'd probably end up having a good time. Alcohol was involved, and people I got along well with were present, but I had a Rose-shaped issue with the whole night.

After our evening talking underneath the bleachers and the incident by the creek, the last thing I needed was to ply myself with alcohol and have her in my path.

I was acutely aware that something had happened between us that night. I wasn't sure what, but it had changed the dynamic.

Now I was in a situation in which 'doing something stupid' seemed almost inevitable. The new cocktail bar Carla hired for the party—The Bobbly Olive—was sleek and well-decorated, with low lighting and music popular with twenty-somethings playing too loudly in the background. Add in deceptively strong cocktails, and you had a recipe for disaster.

I hadn't spotted Rose yet. In any other circumstance, her absence was a blessing. Now it was making me drink more in anticipation of her arrival.

My collar tightened like a noose around my neck. I tugged and shifted the material enough to breathe.

Carla had insisted we dress up for the occasion, which meant it had taken me far too long to get ready. I'd never debated ties or shirts in my life. I was a grab and go guy, but tonight I labored between white shirt and red tie, or gray shirt and black tie. I settled on black shirt and silver tie because the whole experience darkened my mood.

I glanced over at Eli, who had flawless fashion sense, which no one would have guessed if they saw him on a construction site. Owen was more of a traditional dresser rather than fashionable—even now, he wore a shirt, sports coat, tie, and pants, which was more formal than the occasion required. Carla seemed to be relishing it since most of the time he was in jeans and a cotton shirt.

My choice of black was wise. You could never go wrong with black, but I still felt unbelievably self-conscious wearing the damn tie. I downed my drink and headed to the bar, intending to move straight onto the next one.

"Look who's playing into the tall, sexy, and mysterious stereotype," a female voice said to my left; it was Ruthie. Her naturally curly red hair perfectly straightened to compliment her clinging, scarlet dress. Almost everyone would agree that she was a pretty girl, but much cuter than she was sexy. Clearly, she was trying to go for the latter, and it was working well if the looks she was drawing were anything to go by.

I smiled at her. "You look wonderful, Ruthie. Can I buy you a drink?"

"Oh, look at that, my favorite barfly asking the barmaid if she wants a drink. I'll have a Cosmo."

I parroted back the drink order to the barman, adding on an old fashioned for myself.

"What's with the all-black get-up?" Ruth asked as the barman prepared our drinks. "I can't say I dislike it. It's very … unexpected."

"I added a splash of color." Once again, I tugged at my tie.

"Gray isn't a color."

"It's different from black. I didn't know what to wear. I haven't been to a place like this since college, and even then, I preferred going to normal bars given the choice."

"You sound like an old man."

"That hurts." A thump sounded when I hit my chest. "Is it so wrong to know what you like and stick with it?"

She shrugged. "There's nothing wrong with it, but then you might never take any risks that end up paying off. Like this dress, for example." She turned around so I could take in the whole outfit. The dress was backless, like the blue one Rose had shown up to Frazier Falls wearing. Imagining Rose in Ruth's dress sent a flare of heat to my groin.

"What about the dress?" I asked innocently, desperately trying to keep my imagination in check and on Ruthie.

She smirked. "It's not my kind of dress, is it? But it looks great on me. If this place hadn't opened in Frazier Falls, I might never have had the guts to buy it. But now I can see how many guys are looking at me, and I can't wait to wear it the next time I go out with Dan."

"He's the guy from the next town over you've been texting, right?"

Her smile lit up the low-lighted room. "Sure is. It's going well with him, thank God."

The bartender handed us our drinks, and as I took a

welcomed swallow, Eli walked over, his face bright with amusement.

"Guess who walked in, took one look at you laughing away with Ruthie, and grew a face like thunder?"

I didn't need him to answer the question for me. A few days ago, it would have filled me with glee to know Rose was pissed off seeing me easily talking to a woman, but now …

I resisted the urge to shake my head. The two of us had cleared the air. Her seeing me talking with Ruth should have meant nothing. Instead, it made me feel uneasy like I'd done something wrong.

Turning from the bar, I searched for her until a familiar head of blond hair by Carla drew my attention, but the crowded room prevented me from seeing her completely.

"Should I be flirting outrageously with you all night?" Ruthie asked as Eli snorted in laughter.

They both seemed surprised when I shook my head.

"No. We're a little too old to play games, don't you think?"

Eli raised an eyebrow. "I'd have to agree to disagree on that point, but do whatever you want." He looked at Ruthie. "Want to buy me a drink, Ruthie?"

She let out a noise of disbelief. "And have Emily kick my ass? You're on your own."

I moved away from both of them, only realizing when I was halfway across the bar moving toward Rose, I had no idea what I was doing. Carla had spotted me and waved me over, making it too late to change direction.

When I reached the pair, Rose looked away, so I took the opportunity to check her out with a sidelong glance as I greeted Carla.

Rose's dark blond hair was carefully twisted back with the right amount of loose hairs framing her face. Her slip of a dress was pale pink and shiny, somewhat vamped up with black heels, a black choker, and dark red lipstick. When she finally looked at me, her blue eyes didn't show the warmth I'd seen in them only a few nights prior.

"Hi," she murmured before looking away.

"When did you get here?" I asked. "You seem to be pretty fashionably late."

Carla laughed. "Rose would hang her head in shame if she were on time to an event." She glanced at me curiously, as if wondering why I seemed to be talking to Rose but knowing better than to ask. With a not-so-subtle searching look over my shoulder, she excused herself by saying, "It looks like Owen wants me over by the bar."

Her exit left me standing awkwardly at the back of the room with a woman who, for whatever reason, seemed annoyed with me. This only infuriated me in turn, since I hadn't done anything for her to get pissed off about.

"I'm going to—" she searched for an escape, an excuse, anything to save her, but I held out my arm to stop her.

"Are you mad because you saw me laughing with Ruthie at the bar?"

She looked at me, her face blushing underneath her perfectly applied makeup as her eyes widened in horror.

"Who told you that lie?"

I inclined my head in the general direction of Eli, who was currently engaged with a large group of people hanging on his every word. "Eli saw you come in and said you didn't look happy."

She took a long swig from the champagne flute she held. "You were checking her out, and I was …"

"Jealous?"

"No, it's that I've never seen you like that with anyone. It threw me off."

I raised an eyebrow. "I think you believe I'm a virgin, Rose."

"I—of course I don't think that," she spluttered, which

only made her cheeks flush more scarlet. "It's—I've never seen you flirt. And I wasn't mad. I simply didn't want to interrupt you."

"Sure thing," I said, taking her now empty glass before turning to walk toward the bar. She tried to follow me, but I stopped her.

"What are you doing?"

"Getting you a refill." I lifted her empty glass to emphasize my point. "You keep our spot by the wall. God knows it's the only free space of breathable air in this packed room."

Her red lips lifted at the comment as I went about ordering more drinks. Out of the corner of my eye, I noticed both Eli and Owen, along with Carla and a curious Emily, trying to hide the fact that they were watching Rose and me. I rolled my eyes and gave them the finger, getting my drinks from the bartender before heading back to Rose.

When I handed her the glass of champagne, she held it out in a toast.

"What are we celebrating?" I lifted my glass.

"What, you mean other than your big brother and my high school bestie's marriage?" Rose joked. "I don't know ... maybe we're toasting being a little more grownup than we were fifteen years ago?"

I clinked my tumbler against her flute. "I guess I could toast to that."

The lighting of the cocktail bar lit up Rose's little dress with all sorts of colors. It made her look ethereal—like she was made of the lights themselves. When she caught me staring, she lifted a perfectly shaped brow.

"It looks like you are checking *me* out now, Cooper."

"What can I say?" I swallowed down half of my drink before continuing. "You look damn good, Rogers. Though it pains me to admit it."

She smiled devilishly and reached up to tug on the pointed collar of my shirt. "Black's a good color on you."

"Are you sure? That's not what you would have said back in high school."

"Obviously, I didn't know anything back then."

"You would have said it matched my dark soul."

"You were quiet, Paxton, but never mean." She sipped her drink and lowered her head, looking at me from beneath full lashes. "That was my job."

The two of us were startled when someone tripped and fell against my back, pushing me heavily against Rose. With her pinned between my body and the wall, I became acutely and painfully aware of the feeling of having her close to me. How every curve seemed to fit seamlessly against me. Something impossible not to physically react to.

A lurching sensation in my stomach reminded me this situation was the "something stupid" I'd been concerned about earlier.

Funnily enough, it wasn't planned. I had, quite literally, fallen into it.

CHAPTER TWELVE

ROSE

Was it the alcohol? The music? The low lighting? Maybe all of them combined, but having him talk in a low murmur into my ear while the two of us were pressed into the dark corner of the bar caused my stomach to somersault. Back-twisting, double-rolling flips that made me tingly all over.

Without warning, someone bumped into us again, pushing him closer. His stubble grazed the side of my cheek. One of his legs pushed between mine. I didn't know whether I had it in me to look him in the eyes. What was it I wanted to see there?

"You okay?"

I blinked. "What did you say?" My voice was barely audible over the sound of rushing blood in my ears and the pounding music of the bar.

His lips moved closer. "I asked if you were okay. It's busier in here. Seems like half the town is present."

I let out a nervous laugh, which only wavered more when he placed a hand against the wall beside my hip in order to push himself back. "I'm fine, I'm fine," I said, though I certainly didn't feel it.

When he was more than a few inches away from my face, I risked a glance at him. He looked embarrassed, and it was shockingly charming.

"What's wrong?" I wanted nothing more than for his embarrassment to have something to do with me.

He looked away, laughing awkwardly. "It's nothing. It's all the physical proximity and—"

One quick glance below his belt was all I needed to catch his meaning.

"Oh. Oh."

Now, if that wasn't deeply satisfying, then I didn't know what was.

"Make no mistake, this has nothing to do with you being you, Rose," he said, though to my relief, I realized he didn't mean what he said at all.

I quirked an eyebrow. "Oh? Even though you said how great I looked?"

"Anyone can scrub up pretty well if they try hard enough."

"Sure thing. I'm taking your reaction as a compliment, so let's leave it at that."

He blessed me with a goofy grin. Even I could tell he was bordering on tipsy, and I'd never seen the guy drunk in my life.

I felt the same. The champagne made me feel bubbly and bold and forward.

"I didn't mind being pressed against the wall, you know," I said as I closed the gap between us. "I never imagined I'd think of you that way, but there you go."

"Such a charmer."

My fingers danced up his silver tie to tap him on his scruffy chin. "You clearly didn't mind it all that much, either."

There was a moment or two of awkward, charged silence

as we stared at each other, daring the other to make the next move.

Carla appeared at my side, and the moment was gone.

"Is it okay if I steal her for a second, Paxton?" she asked innocently. "I'd like a photo with my bridesmaids."

He smiled easily at her as if we hadn't been engaged in a flustered, adult version of chicken. "Of course not. I never meant to have kept her away from you for so long."

I raised an eyebrow at the comment and walked away. He gave me a half-salute, a devilish smile playing across his lips that made me want to turn around and kiss it off his face.

Guess I was well past the point of pretending I wasn't attracted to him. As Carla handed me another glass of champagne for the photo, Eli's girlfriend, Emily, took the shot. She had a critical eye I appreciated.

"You—the one on the far right—no, I don't remember your name—you're slightly too far away from everyone else. Bloody hell, why are you so rigid? You're not made of wood. Loosen up a little."

I almost broke my perfect photo composure with the need to burst out laughing at her Irish-accented, hilariously blunt comments, but I held it back until the impromptu photo op was finished.

I marched straight over to her afterward. "So, you're Eli's girlfriend?"

She smiled. "I suppose I am. I'm Emily Flanagan."

"Are you related to Judy—the woman my mom's friends with?"

"That would be my ma."

My eyes widened slightly. "But isn't she over seventy?"

Emily nodded. "She had me late. I don't think she ever thought she'd be a mother. I take it Lucy Rogers is your ma? Which would make you—"

"Rose. Yeah, that would be me. Lovely to meet you."

Carla joined us. Her expression was bright and happy and definitely drunk. "I'm so glad the two of you have finally met. All the Coopers are now taken."

Emily looked at me, confused. "Are you with Paxton? I didn't think he had a—"

"Oh, God, no," I exclaimed, glaring at Carla. "Carl's drunk and making fun of me."

"Oh, come on, Rose, you're not that blind," Carla complained. "The guy hasn't stopped eating you with his eyes since I took you away for photos. Whether he wants to admit it or not, he has it bad for you, and I know you feel the same."

"Are you sure it's not the booze speaking?" I joked, avoiding having to respond to her accurate observations. "Say all this again when you're sober and see how well it holds up."

"Challenge accepted." She grabbed a martini from the bar and raised it.

Owen appeared behind her, snaking his arms around her waist as he propped his head on her shoulder. He smiled brilliantly at us.

"May I steal my fiancée, ladies?" he asked sweetly.

"I'd like to steal Emily, too," Eli added as he showed up on Owen's left. Seeing the two of them side by side was strange —they looked so much alike, even taking into account that they were brothers.

Paxton looked like them in many ways, and yet he didn't. He was the fair-haired sexier version.

"I'm sure Pax can keep you company," Carla teased as she was led away. I scowled after her as I downed my champagne.

A couple of hours whiled away as I made idle chat with people I hadn't seen since high school, though my focus was on Paxton the entire time. I instinctively knew where he was in the room at any given moment. I felt him around me.

Considering how many times I caught him looking in my direction, I was certain he knew exactly where I was at all times, too. We were like two storms rotating around each other.

Eventually, we came face to face once more, and I decided to throw all caution to the wind. We were both equally tipsy, and I was only going to be in Frazier Falls for another couple of weeks. He was a perfect distraction from my current disastrous romantic life back in New York.

"Do you want to get out of here?" we said in unison and grinned at each other like the drunk idiots we were.

"Your place?" I suggested.

He nodded, then silently led the way through the throng of people and out onto the street without so much as a goodbye to anyone. The swift exit was much appreciated.

His house was less than ten minutes from the cocktail bar, situated right where the creek began to bend southwards. It was modest in size, but considering I'd spent much of my adult life living in tiny, overly expensive New York apartments, it felt spacious.

"I can't believe you can afford an actual house with a back yard and everything when I can barely afford a one-bedroom apartment in mid-town New York."

"Maybe if you didn't live in the most expensive city in the United States, you could afford something bigger."

"Oh, yeah, because places like Frazier Falls are littered with job opportunities for fashion editors."

He shrugged as he unlocked his front door, letting me in first before following closely behind. "You never know. We have a cocktail bar now. We're very metropolitan."

I let out a burst of laughter at the comment, but before the sound had been fully realized, he slammed me against the now-closed door and kissed me—hard. The sheer force of the action reminded me of when he'd pushed me against that car when he'd been angry. Back then, I hadn't understood why it had excited me so much. Now I did. I pulled away, breathless.

His eyes glinted in the darkness of his hallway.

"What was that for?" I asked.

"I've been wanting to kiss you all night; self-respect be damned."

"You can't admit you're attracted to me without blaming it on some critical lapse in judgment?"

He shook his head. "Nope."

"How about I make that admission a little easier for you?"

With ease, I shrugged out of my satin dress, letting it sweep past my legs to puddle on the hardwood floor. He took in the sight of me in my underwear with hungry eyes.

"If I take off the dress, I'm all in black like you," I murmured, resting my arms on his shoulders and lacing my fingers behind his neck. "Guess we match."

The left side of his mouth quirked up into a half-smile at the comment.

"Maybe for the night."

He unlaced my hands and dropped them from his shoulders, taking hold of one of them as he led me through the darkness to his bedroom.

"For the night sounds good to me, too."

I fell back. My hands reached for his hair, desperately pulling him in close as he fumbled with his jeans. I stifled a laugh as he drunkenly struggled with his tie and the buttons of his shirt, but eventually, he was free of the tie, and his shirt hung open. I let go of his hair in order to run my hands up his chest, finally fulfilling my burning desire to feel his abs beneath my fingertips.

When he tried to shrug off his shirt, he overbalanced and fell off the bed.

"Holy hell." I burst into a fit of giggles as he thumped to

the floor. I rolled over to the edge to see him lying on the hardwood, half-naked and unconscious. He'd knocked himself out cold.

"Paxton?" I murmured, somewhat concerned. I fell off the bed and landed beside him. He was breathing and seemed fine. Running a hand across the back of his head, I felt the slightly raised bump which had likely knocked him out. Sighing heavily, I roped one of his arms around my shoulder and struggled and heaved his massive frame until I got him back on the bed. He stirred enough to say "Ouch" and fell into a deep sleep.

"I can't believe you," I grumbled as I undid the rest of his shirt before throwing the duvet cover over him, climbing to the other side of the bed full of disappointment and worry. "This wasn't where I saw this going." I turned on to my side so I could watch his sleeping face.

I'd wondered earlier about what set him apart from Owen and Eli, and now I knew. I liked the guy. I liked him a lot. It was exactly as Carla had said. I had it bad for him, and I'd had it bad for a long, long time.

CHAPTER THIRTEEN

PAXTON

The quiet but incessant buzz of my cell phone brought me out of a deep sleep. Groggy and confused, I glanced at the screen—it was Sunday, so why did my alarm go off? Except it wasn't the alarm, it was Carla calling.

Swinging myself up into a sitting position, I answered.

"What's up?" I mumbled, yawning in the process. My head throbbed like it had been split in two. "It's barely eight."

"Aww, I'm sorry, Paxton," she replied. "Is Rose with you? I think her cell is dead, and her mom is worried because she didn't come home last night."

I frowned at my phone. "Why on earth would Rose be with me?"

She laughed and then groaned. "Oh, that was bad for my head. Stupid hangover. But you can't be serious? She left with you."

"What do you mean?" Suddenly, someone moaned softly in their sleep behind me, and I felt a body hit my back.

Oh, dear God, no!

"I'll call you back." I hung up before she had a chance to

protest and turned to confirm the person behind me was indeed who I knew it would be—Rose.

"Kill me now," I muttered aloud, not quite sure what I was supposed to do. Was I allowed to wake her up? Did I even want to? What exactly happened between the two of us the night before?

I tried to think, but my head hurt too damn much. Running a hand through my hair, I found a lump the size of Texas on the back of my head. That, along with the copious amount of alcohol I'd consumed the night before, explained the pain I felt.

Stumbling from my bedroom to the bathroom, I located a bottle of painkillers and a glass, which I promptly filled to the brim with water. My throat was a desert landscape complete with a prickly cactus. I sucked the water down like a man who had wandered through the fires of hell for days.

I hung around in the bathroom for longer than necessary, choosing to shower and shave even though handling a razor in my current, hungover state was probably not advisable. What else could I do? She was in my bed, and I had no memory of the night before, which meant I'd have to rely on her telling me the truth. Not her strongpoint.

Whether she chose to tell the truth or to lie, there was absolutely no escaping the fact that she had been asleep in my bed, which meant that, at the least, I'd consented to her being there.

So much for stopping anything stupid from happening, you idiot.

I struggled to recall the night before. There was a memory of getting pushed against her at the cocktail bar, and then Carla took her away for group photos, and then what? My memory of the night after that point was hazy, filled with bits and pieces of unimportant conversations with people from high school and constant glances in her direction.

"Damn," I muttered as I forced my way back to my bedroom, a towel wrapped around my hips. She was still asleep when I sat down beside her. I risked shifting the duvet to see, with relief, that she still had her underwear on. I'd also had my underwear on when I woke up, which suggested we hadn't gotten as far as I'd feared.

My racing heart calmed long enough to look at her sleeping face. Her eye makeup was smudged, as was her lipstick. The same color I'd washed from my face moments ago. Her hair was in disarray, but despite all of that, she was damn beautiful. Almost angelic, though that wasn't a word I'd ever use to describe the woman in front of me.

Ignoring my brain screaming no, I ran a hand over her hair, smoothing it back and away from her face.

She opened her eyes.

"Were you pretending to be asleep?" My hand jerked back so fast it smacked me in the face.

"Obviously," she replied, her voice a little hoarse. She coughed to clear her throat. "I woke up when you hung up the phone." She was once again checking me out. I almost regretted not getting dressed before sitting on the bed —almost.

I fumbled for something to say. "Do you ... do you want some water?"

"Please."

I resisted the urge to flat-out run to the bathroom. When I returned with a full glass and painkillers, she thanked me with a nod before taking both, drinking the water as eagerly as I had done.

With her sitting up in bed, I could see far more of her lacy black underwear and almost cursed when I reacted to it.

She raised an eyebrow. "Something wrong?"

"What happened last night?" I blurted, sitting down to

hide that a lingerie-clad Rose was a sight that turned me on. "We didn't …"

To my surprise, she laughed. "You don't remember?"

I shook my head, which only made her laugh harder.

"We left the bar together around midnight and headed back here. We made it to the bed, and then—"

"Then?"

"You fell off trying to remove your shirt and knocked yourself out." She wiped a tear away from her eye. "I was so angry at first, but honestly, it was hilarious."

"You aren't going to tell anyone, are you?"

"What, and lose the right to lord it over you forever? God no. This is staying between the two of us."

"That simultaneously makes me feel better and worse."

She reined in her laughter. "Do you always act outrageously when you're drunk?"

I shrugged. "Sometimes. When I was working in Aspen Cove with my brothers, we got wasted one night and, apparently, I sang karaoke all night. And danced. And hit on the ex of the guy we were working with."

"Sounds like you know how to handle your liquor."

"Usually I'm fine, but I drank a lot last night. And …"

She quirked a brow. "And?"

I gave her an obvious once-over, which caused her to blush. "And there was a certain someone there that had me on edge the whole night."

"Oh, so you do remember last night?"

"Only bits and pieces. Not much. Not after we were pushed against the wall."

She let the sheet fall to her waist. "It was an interesting night."

I couldn't take my eyes off the alabaster skin of her breasts that spilled over the top of the lacy material. "That's

… one way to put it." I shook my head and stood. "Do you want to use my shower?"

"Yes, if that's okay. Showing up at my mom's looking like this will make her freak."

Her mentioning her mom caused me to reach for my phone and check the time. I swore loudly. "I need to be at your place in half an hour to fix your mom's oven and to cut the grass."

Her mouth twisted and settled into a frown.

"Great. She's going to love the two of us showing up together."

"She'll love it even more if we don't clean ourselves up." I handed her a towel. "Go make yourself decent."

She laughed. "I don't think there's any way I can make last night's outfit look decent." She looked around my room. "Would you get my dress for me?"

I paused before saying, "Your what?"

"My dress. I took it off in the hallway. Right by the front door. You don't remember anything, do you?" She licked her lips. "It's a shame."

I left the bedroom without saying another word, moving down the hallway until I found the incriminating evidence. The shiny pink fabric caught the sunlight streaming into my house, reflecting it back at me. It reminded me of how it had caught the colored lights of the bar, and how beautiful she'd looked wearing it.

I glanced in the direction of the bathroom, where the sound of running water echoed past the closed door. No doubt she looked even better without clothes on.

When I returned to my bedroom, I rummaged through my closet, first getting dressed and then locating a flannel shirt she could wear over her dress. It was definitely too hot outside for it, but it was better than having her walk home nearly naked.

"Better than me having to put up with her wearing it and doing nothing about it," I muttered.

"What did you say?"

I whipped around. She stood in the doorway wrapped in a towel, her skin glistening from the shower. Her face was clear of makeup, and her hair was tied back in a messy bun, yet she somehow looked ridiculously sexy.

I looked away. "I didn't say anything. Here," I said, holding out the shirt for her. "Put this on over your dress."

"You worried about my reputation?"

"Absolutely not. I'm worried about mine."

She burst out laughing. "I suppose I can wear it to make you feel better."

I tossed it into her hands. "Do what you like."

She came around to face me, her lips falling into a pout. "Don't be like that. I was teasing."

With her wet, full lips calling me and big blue eyes staring me down, a droplet of water fell over her collarbone to drip between her towel-encased breasts. I wanted to grab her and throw her on the bed—to show her what I likely would have done had I not fallen into unconsciousness the night before.

Instead, I gave her a small smile. "Get dressed. I'll be late at the rate you're going."

"I'm pretty sure my mom won't care what time you show up if you show up with me."

She turned out to be correct, as demonstrated by the look of sheer glee on Lucy's face when the two of us appeared at her front door together.

"Oh my," she exclaimed, "what have we here? Paxton, were you taking good care of my daughter for me? I was worried about her, you know?" She looked at Rose. "You could have messaged me to say you weren't coming home."

Rose made a face. "I'm not sixteen, Mom. I can stay out all night if I want to."

"You're forgiven since you were with Paxton," Lucy stressed my name as she beamed at me.

"Mom, nothing happened between us," Rose said, though it fell on deaf ears.

"What happens in the bedroom stays in the bedroom. Now, Paxton, would you be a dear and cut the grass first? I swear, it gets so long so quickly now with all this sunshine."

Rose disappeared inside as I headed to the shed to get the lawnmower. It was so hot outside; I ended up pulling off my T-shirt before starting the work, which earned me a whistle of appreciation from Lucy.

"Rose, dear, come sit outside with me when you've changed clothes. The view is spectacular," she called back into the house.

I shook my head at my fate.

What I hadn't expected was Rose to appear in a racy black bikini, which reminded me of the lingerie she'd been wearing last night. Only this had less material. I assumed it was her intention to distract, though the sunglasses she wore hid her expression well.

Her gaze lingered on me. She slid her sunglasses down her nose a little as if appraising me as well. I resisted the urge to look away.

"Rose, I'd hardly call that a bikini," Lucy said, though she didn't sound all that disapproving.

Rose laughed. "Nick sent it over for me—it's part of a swimwear line I was writing an article for. Who am I to say no to free clothes? Besides, I want to tan as much of my skin as possible. If Paxton weren't here, I'd sunbathe naked." She reclined into a lounge chair without another word, crossing her long legs in front of her as she left me with the tantalizing image of her lying naked in the sun.

This was worse than her calling me names.

CHAPTER FOURTEEN

ROSE

"Come on, Paxton, you have to try it. It's so hot out. Maybe you could sit down and join us before you finish? I don't want you collapsing from the heat."

I lie back on one of the loungers as my mom offered him pink lemonade while he staunchly refused. I suppressed a grin. I knew what was going through his head right now—aside from an alcohol-induced migraine—as much as I knew exactly what I was doing to keep those thoughts in his head.

He had passed out on me, and I wanted payback. I wouldn't be able to let this rest until we slept together. Then my curiosity would be satisfied, and I could put all thoughts of him to sleep.

Knowing the conclusion I'd reached the night before when I watched him sleep, I knew I was lying to myself. I didn't want it to be just once, but I couldn't do anything about that right now. Especially not when he seemed horrified by the idea that we'd come close to doing the deed.

What options did I have? All I could do was wear the tiniest bikini I owned and lie out in the sun in front of him as he mowed the lawn—shirtless. It was like the beginning of a smutty B-movie, and I was okay with that.

He ignored me as he mowed over the grass, but I knew he was aware of my presence. I could see it in the way his muscles tensed whenever he passed my line of sight. The way he kept his eyes downcast to make sure he couldn't accidentally sneak a peek.

I'd seen the way he looked at me when I'd shown up in the garden wearing a piece of floss and two pasties. I didn't imagine I had to do much more to crumble his resolve.

I never would have thought this kind of teasing would be possible with him, but I was enjoying it immensely.

My phone buzzed to life now that I'd charged it, and a hoard of notifications bombarded the device. Most of them were from Carla, wondering where I'd gone the night before, followed by outrageous and delighted comments about how people had spotted Paxton and me leaving the cocktail bar at the same time. She naturally put two and two together and had reached the conclusion we'd slept together.

It's what we had intended to do, and she'd never believe me if I said he knocked himself out, anyway.

I replied to her barrage of messages by saying that I had stayed the night at his house, leaving no further comment for her to interpret. I knew it would drive her mad, which caused me to smile. Carla would demand details over the next few days, so it wouldn't hurt her to wait a little longer.

Other notifications were photos being posted from the previous night, including a candid one of Paxton and me laughing at something he'd said, and he had a sexy smirk on his face.

To the unknowing, we looked like a couple.

I glanced up from my phone to look at the real thing.

God, he looked great working on the lawn. His skin, with its light sheen of sweat, glistened in the sunlight. Whenever his hair fell into his eyes, he paused to push it away from his forehead. His muscles rippled when he stretched, and I couldn't tear my eyes away. What kind of self-respecting, hot-blooded female had that kind of control? Not me.

My mom sat beside me, pushing me for details about the night before. Eventually, it got to be a little too much. I unlocked my phone and tried to engage in a text conversation with Nick, but I was distracted by the sight in front of me. Knowing he would be delighted with the gesture, and more than a little jealous, I took a photo of Paxton and sent it to Nick.

He looked up when he realized a phone was pointed in his direction, frowning slightly as he held a hand up to shield his eyes from the sun. I grinned at him unapologetically, shrugging my shoulders as if I were saying, "What did you expect?"

He shook his head at my shamelessness, but he smiled.

As he seemed to finish cutting the grass, I became worried that my skin would burn. I hadn't put sunblock on in my haste to get outside and flaunt in front of him, and I didn't want that to bite me in the ass so close to Carla's wedding.

With reluctance, I moved back inside, heading upstairs to my bedroom to inspect my skin in my full-length mirror. I hadn't burned, which was great, but I was too close to risk going back outside without putting on sunblock and letting it soak into my skin.

That meant I couldn't put it on while I was outside and make him watch. I shouldn't have been so quick to go outside in the first place, but then I remembered him mentioning that he was fixing my mom's oven after mowing the lawn, which meant he'd be in the kitchen for a while.

A small smile curled my lips. I removed my bikini and put on a deep blue, short silk kimono that I'd ordered online.

There were little shorts that were supposed to be worn with it, but the robe itself was long enough for me to get away with wearing it alone.

Playing with my hair until it was artfully tousled, I opened my bedroom door and walked right into Paxton.

"Holy hell," I called out as he said something similar. I took a step back in order to look at him, only to find him staring right down the front of my kimono, which had loosened when I ran into him.

"I was using the bathroom," he mumbled. His eyes moved back to mine, watching me intently.

"What is it you're looking for when you stare at me like that?" I dared to take another step backward to see if he would follow.

He did.

I took another, then another, until he stood on the threshold of my bedroom.

"I don't know what I'm looking for," he admitted.

"I don't think you'll know until you let this happen."

"Maybe I don't want to know."

I laughed. "You definitely wanted to know last night."

"We were drunk."

"And you couldn't take your eyes off me this morning, either." I let the kimono slip off my shoulder, satisfied to see his heated gaze flicker as he watched the movement of the fabric before locking eyes with me again.

"I'd have acted like that with any hot woman wrapped in a towel in my bedroom." His words stung until I realized he was lying. The lie showed in his eyes, which had turned a stormy blue.

"Bullshit. If I were another hot woman, then you would have slept with me last week when I got into town, and that would be it. No. The reason you're acting like this is because it's me."

There was an agonizing pause where it seemed as if he might deny it—might shatter my belief, but then he took a step forward, sliding his hands across the silky fabric at my waist as he closed the gap between us. He rested his forehead on mine, his intense eyes looking at me like I'd never seen them look at a person before.

Only look at me like that. Leave this Paxton for me.

"Fine," he said simply and quietly. "You win."

His mouth was on mine as he lifted me one-armed off the floor, using his other to close my bedroom door behind us before pulling the kimono from my body.

His hands were all over me as I nimbly undid the buttons of his jeans, pushing them down as he kicked his shoes off.

We barely reached the bed before he was in me. This was not the time or place for us to slowly explore each other's bodies. No, this was the time for us to fulfill an aching, swelling desire for each other as quickly and as desperately as possible.

Whatever this was could be ironed out later.

CHAPTER FIFTEEN

PAXTON

I'd been possessed from the moment she barged into me wearing that blue robe. The next fifteen minutes had been a rush of sensations and actions that were both incredibly vivid and blurry at the same time. Bad choices. Intense feelings.

I couldn't believe it. I'd had sex with Rose Rogers. Of my own free will. And, despite how much better for me it would have been if it had been terrible, it wasn't. It was the exact opposite of terrible. It was life-altering, which meant I was desperate to do it again.

The two of us lay on our backs, breathing heavily when she rolled over to look at me.

"You look annoyed."

"I'm annoyed it was good."

"Most people wouldn't be annoyed that sex for the first time with someone was good. Generally, it's awkward and less than expected."

"Guess I'm a weirdo then."

She sighed as she rolled onto her front, running a hand

through my hair as she gently kissed my lips. It set my heart running.

"I think you could do with being more honest with yourself, Mr. Cooper."

"What, and have no impulse control like you?"

"It certainly didn't hurt you today, did it?" she laughed. "Come on, Pax, there's no way you can regret something happening that felt that damn great, and you know it."

I stiffened underneath her hand as she trailed it across my chest. She had never called me by my nickname before. It made me feel odd. I wasn't sure how to describe it. Like by allowing her to use it, I would be accepting her connection to me. Considering what had happened between us, I supposed she was linked to me, but it still felt weird.

Thinking about how different things were between us, I placed one of my hands over hers. "Yeah, you're right," I finally agreed. "That felt pretty damn great."

She planted little kisses down my neck to my collarbone. The light touch tickled me, causing bumps to rise across my skin.

"I wouldn't be opposed to another, altogether slower round two," she murmured, her voice low and sexy as hell.

I groaned. "If I don't get downstairs soon and fix your mom's oven, she'll have cause to come up here to find out what's going on. Do you want to have to explain this to her?" I asked, waving a hand in the general direction of the two of us.

"I guess not." She swung up and out of bed, grabbing a pair of shorts and a camisole from her closet. "I'll be in the bathroom cleaning up. You know your way downstairs." She gave me another slow sensual kiss before walking away.

I shook my head. The woman was a damn vixen. She was a nuisance, but I was ready to dive into her kind of trouble again.

She disappeared to the bathroom, leaving me to find my forgotten jeans, shoes, and underwear on the floor. I was about to leave her bedroom when I noticed photos attached to the mirror of her vanity table. Curious, I wandered over to look.

Most were what I would have expected—a teenage Rose posing with her friends while someone took an overexposed Polaroid, but there were a few that surprised me. She had a couple of both the Rogers and Coopers together. I assumed it was because of how happy her parents looked in them, but there on the floor of one of the photos was a young Rose and a slightly older me. She was tugging at my hair while I sat there passively taking the torment.

I snorted in laughter. I looked ridiculous, and she looked annoyed. If our genders were reversed, I would have assumed it was a typical case of a boy picking on the girl he liked.

I paused, considering the thought. Though it wasn't impossible that was the case with her and me—that she picked on me because she liked me—a large part of me found it difficult to believe. She had made her dislike of me perfectly clear as we grew up, and then she ignored me altogether in high school. That wasn't the mark of someone with a crush.

Another photo caught my eye. It was the same high school junior and senior photo that had been posted online a few days prior—the one I'd been mulling over in bed. There she was, standing at the front in her cheerleader uniform, and there I was standing in the back trying to blend in with the background.

She had circled my figure in the photo, scribbling beside it something that looked an awful lot like the word idiot. If I had been laughing at the photo before, I was absolutely howling at this one. So much for her growing up. Even when she'd reached her final years of high school, she still couldn't help but vocalize her aversion to me.

"Why are you cracking up?" she asked, suddenly appearing behind me.

"I'm laughing at you," I admitted, gesturing to the photos.

Her face paled before flushing a furious scarlet. "Oh my—oh my God, why would you look at those? They're private."

"They're hardly private if they're on show in a room you invited me into." Her mouth opened and shut like a fish gulping air as she realized she couldn't argue her case.

"I can't believe you did this." I pointed at the circle around me in the photo. "What was the point? For all intents and purposes, you ruined the photo for display."

She rolled out her bottom lip and stretched it into a thin line. "I felt like it was an improvement. I should have scribbled you out."

"Charming. What caused you to write I was an idiot on it in the first place?"

"I—I'm not sure," she admitted. "You were leaving school for college, so I don't have a clue what you could have possibly done for me to write that. Oh—"

"Oh?" I echoed, raising an eyebrow when she paused mid-sentence.

She giggled. "My friend Nicki had asked you to prom. You refused. I had no idea why you'd say no to her. It's not like you had any other offers, and she liked you, though God knows why. It was better than a pity date. You kind of broke her heart."

I frowned as I tried to remember her friend. "I didn't go to prom," I said as I pulled at the memory, forcing it out. "I told her that I had no intention of going, and she got upset."

Rose looked surprised. "Wait, you actually spoke to her? I always assumed you ignored her request."

"What would you have had me do, walk away from her

when she asked me directly?" I asked, incredulous at how low her opinion of me had been. "Of course, I declined her offer—with words."

"I never got why she liked you in the first place."

"That's because you hated me."

"I never hated you," she complained. "You … annoyed me. A lot."

"Clearly," I replied, glancing at the photo of us as children.

She chuckled. "I told you before, I didn't understand why you wouldn't talk to me. I thought we'd gotten past that."

I shook my head. "We have. Mostly. It's funny to see it with my own eyes. Maybe I deserved all your teasing."

"Well, I certainly thought so at the time."

"But not now?"

"No, not now. Besides"—she sidled up to me, placing a hand on my bare stomach, a mere inch or two above the waistband of my jeans—"there are more interesting ways to tease you as an adult."

I glanced down. "I'm not sure if that's worse."

"Worse for who?"

I leaned over and kissed her. "Me. I don't like you having this much of an effect on me."

Her lips curled into a smile beneath my own. "At least you're admitting to it. And in full disclosure, I wasn't happy she asked you to prom."

"Jealous?"

She half shrugged. "Oh please. Get over yourself." She glanced back at the photo, and I saw the regret in her eyes.

"Unbelievable. You had a secret crush on me."

"Hardly, but now that we've moved past all this, can we behave for Owen and Carla's wedding?"

I brushed my lips against her cheek to whisper into her ear, "What exactly do you mean by behave? Something tells me what you're hoping for is anything but."

"You've figured me out," she murmured. "But I don't want to do anything you're not up for. There's no point in this if you don't want it to happen."

"And if I say I don't?"

She pulled away to stare at me. "Then, you'll be lying because you were definitely up for it." Her eyes went straight to my package.

"Tell me you loved it, and I'll consider being up for it again," I joked, though I slid my hands around her waist as I did.

"Don't act like this is a chore for you."

I adjusted my growing length. "It's a damn hardship."

"Hilarious. Don't forget you still need to fix that oven for my mom."

I pulled away from her as if I had been burned, cursing slightly as I made for the door.

"Why did you distract me for so long?" I complained as I made my way down the stairs with her following closely behind me.

"You should know by now," she said.

"Rose Rogers likes me."

Lucy stood in the kitchen when we reached it. She raised an eyebrow at me—a gesture which reminded me so much of her daughter—then she laughed softly.

"The two of you are like little kids around each other. It's refreshing."

"I'd hardly say we were like kids, Mom," Rose said as she grabbed a can of soda from the fridge, throwing it to me without even asking if I wanted it. I did, but that was beside the point. She was in my head now.

"Oh, nonsense. Running down the stairs arguing with each other; if that's not acting like children, then I don't know what is. Never mind all that fuss in the garden trying to get each other's attention."

I looked away as she stared at her mother. The woman was too sharp for her own good. I had no doubt she knew exactly what the two of us had been up to while we were gone.

"Paxton," Lucy continued, "your T-shirt is still outside. I didn't know if you'd want to put it back on before having a look at the oven?"

I shook my head and smiled at Rose. Two could play her game. "No point in getting it dirty. What seems to be the problem with the oven?"

I whiled away the next hour in silence. Both Rose and her mother left me alone while I got to work. This surprised me, especially after what had happened upstairs.

Was this my life now? Wondering if Rose would hang around and bother me because she could and because she knew it affected me? I had to admit that it didn't sound unpleasant.

I glanced through the kitchen door down the hallway to the open front door. Rose was sitting on the doorstep talking away happily with her mother, not a care in the world as she laughed and complained and told her mom about the latest issue released of the magazine she worked for.

It suddenly occurred to me that she had arrived in Frazier Falls much earlier than planned, and I'd never found out why. Looking at her with her mother, I reasoned that she must have missed home even if she spent half her time complaining about the place. Would she ever consider coming back? *No way.* That magazine said everything about her. It wasn't what was honest and true, but how she could make things look that mattered.

I shook my head to get rid of the thoughts. Her life didn't concern me. I had to be sure it remained that way for my own sanity.

CHAPTER SIXTEEN

ROSE

"What'll it be, ladies?" I arrived at Reilly's ready to drink, but Carla had other ideas.

"Coffees, for now, John."

"Nonsense. You're in the final stages of planning your wedding—surely some mimosas are in the cards?"

Carla laughed. "You trying to compete with The Bobbly Olive?"

From behind the bar, John waggled his finger knowingly. "I always knew how to make good cocktails, Carl. I think you've all been spending too much time with beer and whiskey drinkers in here and have forgotten that I can make any drink you want. I spent my twenties working on a cruise ship, you know."

I widened my eyes. "No way. I never had you pegged for a cruise ship guy." Thinking of old John as Mr. Love Boat made me giggle.

"Maybe you should spend more time getting to know your barman," he replied, a twinkle in his eye. "Might be he's actually the most interesting guy in town, instead of those Coopers."

Emily, who, despite not being one of Carla's bridesmaids, had become part of the bridal party, looked at the man with disbelief. "I seem to recall you pushing me onto them when I first came home to look after my ma."

He shrugged. "It's not like I could be with all of you lovely ladies, though that's a damn shame."

We all laughed. Carla's other two bridesmaids—friends from college—were running late, having been on bachelorette planning duty. I still couldn't believe it was less than a week to the party, and ten days to Carla's big day.

"Are you still set on those coffees, Carl?" John asked, smiling. "Or are you upgrading them?"

She glanced at Emily and me before breaking out into a grin. "Okay. You've twisted our arms. Upgrade away."

I wasn't complaining about the change from caffeine to alcohol. A couple of days had passed since I'd slept with Paxton, and while the two of us had noncommittally messaged each other over the past forty-eight hours, we hadn't met up in person. I hoped that we would, but at the same time, somewhat dreaded it. Was round one a fluke and round two would be a disappointment? Not possible.

The more time I spent with him, the more I realized how much I liked him, and that scared me. I had a life in New York I'd be happy to get back to after Carla's wedding. The last thing I needed was an attachment to Paxton. He was a complication I wasn't prepared to face.

New York and Frazier Falls weren't too far away. If he and I were inclined to see each other on a regular basis, it was under four hours on a plane. We could travel every few months if we chose. It wasn't like I would never be back here. It was simply that I was usually only here for a couple of days at a time to see my mom. Spending time with Paxton would make good use of my often-neglected vacation days.

I laughed at the notion. Was I trying to plan out a long-term arrangement with a guy I wasn't even sure would want to sleep with me again? No doubt he wanted to, but with Paxton, that didn't mean he would. After everything that had happened, there was still a reluctance there—I saw it plain as day when I shortened his name the way his brothers did. He wasn't sure if he wanted to let me in.

He was entitled to those feelings because I hadn't exactly made life easy for him back when we were kids. Even if he had forgiven me, he was allowed to be cautious and should be cautious.

We had agreed to our own version of behaving in the run-up to the wedding, which for me included getting into bed with him again. Now the ball was in his court. If it was going to happen again, it would be up to him. No way would I throw myself at him in desperation. I still had my pride.

At least when I'm sober. I sipped on my mimosa, forcing my attention back to Carla. We were here to finalize a few details for her wedding, and I needed to listen.

"And with that, we're done," she said. "I can happily move on to the far more interesting topic of conversation like what is Rose thinking about right now? My bet is on a Cooper brother, and it's not Owen or Eli."

"Do we have to talk about that?" I complained.

She nodded enthusiastically enough to make her curly hair bounce. "Absolutely. You've been cagey with the details, so you bet your ass you're telling Emily and me what happened."

I glanced at Emily. "Are you at all interested in this?"

She laughed. "I do happen to like Paxton, so I have to admit I'm curious to learn about the kind of woman he's into."

I made a face. "I wouldn't know. I think I'm a weird exception for him."

"Because you went to school together?"

I shook my head. "No. Well, yes we went to school together, but I think it's more the—"

"Incessant teasing and name-calling," Carla cut in. She explained my history with Paxton to Emily in a few succinct sentences.

Emily narrowed her eyes. "Please tell me you apologized for acting like that as a kid."

"I did." I sighed. "It was like shoving a golf ball through a Coke bottle to do it, but I did. I think he and I are finally on even footing."

"You did sleep with him, right?" Carla asked, smirking.

"There was no sleep." I looked away. "And it didn't happen after your cocktail party. It was the next day."

Carla's and Emily's faces lit up with interest. "How did that happen?" Emily asked. "I mean, didn't the two of you go home together?"

"How could you not get it on after the party?" Carla asked incredulously. "You hardly stopped staring at each other the entire night. You were like kindling and flame." Her hands burst into the air. "Explosive."

"It's a long story, but we didn't sleep together until he came around to help my mom out."

"So … how was it?" Carla tossed back her mimosa and held up her glass for another.

"Fast," I admitted. "We were both riled up. But it was great. Pretty damn great."

Carla's brows disappeared under the sweep of her bangs. "You only did it once?"

I nodded. "He still had to fix the oven, and my mom was home. We didn't want to raise suspicion, not that she didn't work out what was going on anyway."

"Are you gonna keep hooking up while you're back here?" Emily asked. "You are going back to New York after the wedding, aren't you?"

I nodded again. "Yeah, I'm going back, and I don't know if we'll hook up again, to be honest."

"But you want to," Carla added.

Everything inside me reacted to the thought. "Obviously."

She laughed at that. "Obviously? See, I said you had it bad for him. You never wanted to admit it back when we were teenagers."

"Shut up. It's mortifying to think that all this time, I actually liked him. Ugh, it's disgusting."

"You sure you're not the weird one instead of him?"

"That possibility makes it worse."

We were interrupted when Carla's brother Rich entered the bar. He saw the three of us, smiled brightly, and then approached. "I'm only in to drop something off. See you at home, Carl." He was in and out of the bar in a matter of seconds after handing something over to John.

Seeing the man in question reminded me of what my mom had said about Rich, and how Nick had asked if there were any not so straight men in Frazier Falls who'd be at Carla's wedding.

"Carla," I murmured, keeping my voice low. She and Emily immediately sidled in closer like I was giving out state secrets. "For reasons I shall keep private for now, but which definitely involve my mom being a busybody, I can't help but ask…"

She glanced at the door, then back at me. "Is this about Rich? You trying to set him up?"

I bit my lip as I wondered how to word my question. "Kind of. Maybe. Um … is he straight? I realized that I don't know."

Carla held a hand to her mouth as if to stop herself from laughing out loud. She glanced at John behind the bar before replying, "I don't know, either. I mean, I know of a couple girls he's slept with, and he went out with someone in college, but he always referred to the person in neutral terms. To this day, I have no idea if it was a guy or a girl."

"He might not be." Nick would be so excited if that was the case.

She shrugged. "It's not something I'd ever push for him to talk about. If he wants to discuss it with me, then I'd be happy to lend an ear, but it's his personal life. All I want is for him to be happy. I don't care who he loves."

"I agree wholeheartedly." I tucked the idea away. "I didn't mean to intrude by asking. I think my mom got into my head."

She laughed softly. "You still put too much stock into what other people say and think. Ah, well, at least you're not as bad as you were back when we were kids."

I narrowed my eyes. "What do you mean by that?"

"Oh, you can't possibly act innocent over this. You literally joined the cheerleading team because someone mentioned you'd look cute in the outfit. You didn't even like the squad."

"Okay, that's one thing, but I did look cute in the outfit, so—"

"You distanced yourself from me for a while when the squad told you it was weird that all I did was hang out with boys."

"I already apologized to you about that in senior year," I complained, feeling put-out. "Do I not get credit for that?"

"Naturally. Why else would you be sitting here?" she said soothingly. Then she continued. "You went out with Liam Potts because Nicki told you that you'd make the most amazing couple. In reality, she wanted to make sure you were taken, so you didn't ask Paxton to prom. You totally fell for it."

I looked at her in shock. "Seriously?"

Carla shrugged. "Nicki was insecure, and she'd always

liked Paxton, even when we were in elementary and middle school. Come on, don't you remember how jealous of you she was because you were spending all that time with him as kids?"

"I was making fun of him."

"Yes, but you still got to spend time with him because your families were friends. I remember Nicki egging you on to be meaner to him in middle school, too. She must have done it so the two of you would hate each other."

"I …" I didn't know what to say. If this was all true, then not only did I have to reassess half of the decisions I'd ever made in my life, but I also had to face the fact that I had been manipulated into making Paxton's life a misery for someone else's benefit.

"Nicki's a bitch," I muttered, finally.

"Now you get why she wasn't invited to the wedding." Carla rubbed her hands together like she was dusting them off. "I never liked her. She was two-faced and precisely the reason I preferred hanging out with the boys in school than the girls. You would have been a whole lot better off if you'd done the same."

Emily looked at me sympathetically. "There's no need to question your entire life because of this. Carla's clearly trying to get a rise out of you. You're happy with your life the way it is now, right?"

I nodded. "My job and stuff, yeah, but the guy I'd been dating in New York. I wonder if I'd have ever given him the time of day if he wasn't well-connected. I was never a leader but a part of the herd. Why is it I'm only realizing it now?"

Carla frowned. "Because I'm not the kind of friend to blow smoke up your ass."

"Honesty hurts."

"I thought you said you'd never have guessed James was playing you until you saw it with your own eyes?"

John dropped off another round of drinks and disappeared.

"I might have been able to read him better if I'd spent more time with the guys in high school," I murmured. "Maybe I'd have worked out how terrible he was before he broke my heart."

"You don't seem so broken-hearted to me," Emily commented.

"That's only because—"

I paused. I didn't want to say it was because of Paxton, even though I knew that was the truth.

Both Carla and Emily didn't need me to finish my sentence to know what I was going to say.

I glanced at John and raised my drink. "Thanks, John, I needed this."

"That was obvious," he shot back.

I stared into my drink. Why was my life so obvious to others and so confusing to me?

CHAPTER SEVENTEEN

PAXTON

"Remember when I said my house was getting too small for all of us to hang out in? I was being serious."

"Aww, come on, Owen. Yours is the biggest one."

"Has Carla been bragging again?" He waggled his brows in a ridiculous way.

Carla and Rich were sprawled on one end of the sofa nearest the empty fireplace.

Emily and Eli were on the other sofa, and Owen and I were leaning against the breakfast bar, opening fresh beers.

He clinked his bottle against mine. "I hear you've been seeing a lot of Rose lately. I was wondering what was going on at the cocktail party."

"You're not supposed to tell our secrets." Carla threw a sofa cushion at him, which only made me laugh harder.

"What did Rose say to you, Carla?" I asked, trying to keep my tone light.

"Are you worried she was disappointed, Pax?" Eli teased. "She always did have high standards."

"You be quiet," Emily scolded him, holding a finger to Eli's lips before kissing them.

"She didn't tell me much of anything," Carla admitted, which immediately set my heart at ease. "I figured some stuff out. Rose is pretty easy to read."

"Quite an unpleasant woman," Eli muttered.

Carla didn't have another cushion to throw at him, so she glared in his direction instead. "Rein in your man Emily, or the guys will have to take him out to the woodshed."

"How could you end up being friends with her for this long?" Rich asked his sister, chuckling. "You had one female friend, and almost everyone hated her? Seems bizarre."

Carla shrugged. "Rose rubs people the wrong way, but deep inside, she's a good person. Aren't we all misunderstood at one time or another?"

"She's not exactly who I made her out to be all those years ago." How was it that a few days had erased years of torment? It was probably the sex. Great sex was like a magic elixir to all the world's problems. Make love, not war was a perfect tagline for world peace.

Eli, Owen, and Rich looked at me in surprise. Only Carla and Emily seemed unfazed. Clearly, Emily was in the vote for Rose camp. What was it about weddings that made all the women become matchmakers?

My cell phone buzzed in my pocket, and I pulled it out to distract myself from talking about Rose. Speak of the devil, and she shall appear. She wanted to know what I was up to, and I knew what that meant. More magic elixir was coming my way if I played my cards right.

I desperately wanted to excuse myself from Owen's house to see her, to tear her clothes from her body, to spend time exploring her the way I hadn't had time to yet, but something stopped me.

All around, the extended Cooper family turned to

another topic of conversation, which allowed me to mull over whether I should reply to her text.

If I had another one or two beers, I would definitely tell her to come over to my house. I wasn't stupid enough to not see that happening. I glanced at the bottle in my hand. Was I prepared to give up the beer in case?

It wasn't as if sleeping with her again would be a mistake. We were adults having consensual sex. So why was I finding it so difficult to text her back? I'd always assumed she was the prideful one, but clearly it was me.

I feared if I gave in to my desire for her again, then I would lose for sure. Sleeping with her once felt like an allowable lapse in judgment. Sleeping with her twice ... that was a conscious choice, but was it wise?

I swallowed the groan that inched up my throat. No one needed to know I was currently suffering from a stupid, internal struggle, one that pitted my brain, my heart, and my body against each other.

Owen moved from my side to discuss some ecological urban planning details with Emily, so I chose to sit on the floor by Rich and Carla.

Rich glanced down at me with a frown on his face. "You seem quieter than usual, Pax. Is something wrong?"

Carla smiled. "I bet I can guess what's wrong. It wouldn't have anything to do with Rose, would it?"

Leave it to Carla to hit the bullseye. "Things were much easier when you weren't getting married."

"Falling in love does stupid shit to people. Try it sometime. You might like it." She kicked out her feet and set them on the coffee table. "Maybe if you didn't keep ignoring her, you wouldn't be bothered by her."

"She's like a bad hangover." Was it possible to ache all over from a woman?

"Hair of the dog," Carla tossed back.

I raised an eyebrow. "What has she told you?"

"I already said she hasn't told me anything, but she's been restless and easily frustrated the last few days. It doesn't take a genius to work out why."

A sigh slipped out. "I don't know what to do," I admitted.

"You like her, don't you?" Rich added in. "What's the problem? This all seems needlessly complicated."

"Exactly," Carla said. "Which is why—"

She was interrupted by the doorbell. Since Owen was in the middle of discussing work plans with Emily, and nobody else made any effort to get up, I moved to answer it.

The last thing I expected was for Rose to be at the door. Frozen to the spot where I stood, I unabashedly stared at her.

"You were here, huh?" A flash of disappointment crossed her face. "You could have messaged me back saying you were busy."

"I—you didn't come here to see me?"

She let out a bark of laughter. "I didn't even know you were here."

"Who—"

"Oh, is that Rose?" Carla called out from behind me. I figured out exactly what was happening. "I'm so happy you weren't busy," she said to her friend, happily pushing me out of the doorframe to let Rose in. "Didn't seem right that all the groomsmen were together, and I didn't have one single bridesmaid to keep me company."

Rose smiled awkwardly as Carla led her into the living room. "Where are your college friends, Carl?"

"Staying at Reilly's hotel. I think they experienced a few too many mimosas, so they're already asleep."

"Here's hoping they last through the night on your wedding day."

Carla laughed. "They sure as hell better. You want a

beer?" She pushed at her brother. "Rich, get up, let Rose and Pax have the sofa. We've been hogging it."

Rich grinned at me as he moved.

"No beer for me," Rose said. "I'm not a fan."

"Ah yeah, I almost forgot. What about a vodka cranberry?"

Rose's eyes lit up. "I'll have one of those if you don't mind."

"How's little Rose doing?" Eli asked, grinning in that way he did when he was hoping for some gossip. "I'm afraid none of us got to catch up all that much with you at The Bobbly Olive." He glanced at me and continued. "You were preoccupied in the dark corner."

She blushed. "I've been doing well in New York, thanks. Working as a fashion editor."

"Any significant others we should know about?"

"No," she muttered as Carla handed her a drink.

"That's good," Owen said, smiling. "What's the fun of having someone back in New York who you can't bring home with you to Frazier Falls?"

She seemed to grow a little sad at that, and I wondered why. I felt her arm stiffen beside mine. Worried, I risked grazing the edge of my hand against her skin. Her face warmed up immediately, and then it was as if the sadness had never been there at all.

"Better to be single when you come home for a wedding, anyway," Eli remarked, casting an obvious sidelong glance at me in the process, "in case, you know?"

Emily elbowed him in the ribs. "Stop interfering."

The conversation continued in much the same manner for a while, the entire group falling into easy chatter that caused the woman sitting beside me to relax.

As time wore on, I became increasingly aware of her presence beside me. The flouncy dress she wore showed off her amazing legs, which had caught enough of the sun to have a burnished glow. I had to resist the urge to slide a hand beneath the fabric and up her thigh.

She caught all of my glances, her cheeks blushing more scarlet as it became apparent what I was thinking about. As if to taunt me, she shifted, revealing even more of her skin.

Each glance and touch only increased my desire for her. The twitch in my jeans created the worst situation possible, so I stood up abruptly and turned to her.

"It's way too hot in here. Want to join me outside for some fresh air?"

She agreed without a hint of hesitation. Not a single person in the room said anything.

Eli's shoulders shook with a silent laugh, but he kept his mouth shut as I led Rose out the sliding patio doors of the house into the forest.

When we were out of sight, I twisted a hand through her hair and brought her lips to mine, pulling her against me as my back crashed against the trunk of a tree.

She paused only to artfully peek at the show homes that stood a few yards away. "Would it be better to go in one of them?" she asked, breathless.

"No." I was too impatient already. I didn't have it in me to carefully break into one of the houses.

My response seemed to flip a switch in her. She threw her arms around my neck and her legs around my waist. My fingers slid down to support her, pressing against the skin of her thighs as she moaned into my mouth.

"I wanted to take our time the second time we did this, but I don't think I can wait," she murmured.

"Neither can I."

We didn't even undress. All it took was the unbuttoning of my jeans and pushing her panties to the side, and we were ready. She muffled a cry of surprise against my neck as I entered her.

I turned us around to press her against the tree, all the better to gain purchase and rock into her as she desperately clung to my shoulders and neck and hair, kissing me with such passion my lips would be swollen when she was done with them.

When we finished and returned to Owen's living room, Rose made her excuses and left as quickly as possible.

Everyone looked at me.

"Didn't know you had it in you, Pax," Eli joked. "In the forest? I mean, Owen got close when he and Carla almost did it in the creek, but you went and did it in the forest."

"Actually, we did it in the forest, too," Carla smirked as her face grew red. "Several times."

Eli burst out laughing. He looked at Emily, an eyebrow raised.

"Don't even think about it," she threw back.

"I think I'll head off, too," I said. "That woman wears me out."

"I wonder why," Owen called out as I left. I didn't care about their jibes because I knew there was absolutely no shadow of a doubt that I wanted what was going on with me and Rose to be more than what it was, and nothing terrified me more.

CHAPTER EIGHTEEN

ROSE

Before I knew it, Carla's bachelorette party had crept up on me. Owen's party was happening at the same time. With Frazier Falls being a small town, I had no doubt I'd run into a certain Cooper brother at some point or another since the bachelor party was happening a few doors down at Reilly's.

I hadn't seen Paxton since we'd had sex in the forest outside Owen's house. Thinking about it caused my face to burn. I'd never been so bold before, and I didn't think I'd have ever been able to do that with anyone else. With Paxton, everything was different. With him, it was … natural. The word made me laugh, considering where we'd had sex. Can't get much more natural than a forest.

Nick arrived at Reilly's in time to start the party, which would move to The Bobbly Olive once the Cooper brothers got there. He had spent the last hour schmoozing everyone with well-placed comments that were designed to flatter. There was something to be said about our line of work—though people would assume we were overly critical about the way someone looked, we also knew how to find the one thing that worked on a person and make sure they knew how excellent that choice had been.

That was precisely how he had managed to get the bridal party to fall in love with him in under sixty minutes. I had a solid feeling he wouldn't have to buy himself a drink for the rest of the night.

"Why are all the good ones taken or gay?" one of Carla's other bridesmaids, Vanessa, complained. "You're handsome, employed, a sharp dresser and funny. What's not to love?"

"Yes, well, we all can't be me." He looked around the bar. "Eat your hearts out." Nick crooned, and I pretended to vomit. He snorted in laughter as he came over and slung an arm around my waist.

"Unfortunately, Vanessa," Nick continued, his tone merry and remorseful at the same time, "if I were in any way attracted to women, then Rosie right here would be the only one for me."

"Shut the hell up with that 'Rosie' crap, Nick," I admonished. "You sound like my mom. Or, ugh, James."

"See, that's the comment that warrants vomiting, not mine."

I burst out laughing. "You have that right."

"He's still been asking after you, you know. He managed to get Denise into his good graces and has been siphoning information off her about what you're up to."

"Is this James, the scum-bag ex?" Carla asked, suddenly appearing from behind Nick with glasses of champagne in hand for us. She passed them over to a general murmur of thanks.

Nick nodded. "Yes, James, the scum-bag ex. Rose, if you'd actually married him, you'd be Rose Rivers. That sounds ridiculous."

"What, you mean even more ridiculous than, say, Rose Rogers?" There's nothing as nice as a little alliteration. Made everything roll off the tongue. I'd have liked to shout a few others out like Jackass James or Bastard Brady, but all I could think about was Perfect Paxton.

"Ooh, touché. Well done."

"Do you know what would sound pretty great, though?" Carla gave me a side-eye.

Groaning, I shook my head. "Don't say it. Don't—"

"Rose Cooper."

"You're impossible." The whole idea was ridiculous, but I couldn't help but warm to the fact that it didn't sound completely dreadful.

"Can't say it doesn't sound good." Carla sipped her champagne and smiled.

I rolled my eyes, but Nick had attached himself to the new topic of conversation. If anything, Nick was like Velcro when he wanted to be.

"You know she sent me a photo of that Paxton guy shirtless?" He pulled out his phone to search for it until I shoved it down and told him to put it away.

Carla laughed in disbelief. "No way."

"Yes, way. He was all hot and bothered and—"

"He was mowing the lawn," I interrupted. "And though I admittedly sent it to make you jealous, that doesn't mean I want to marry the guy."

"But then we'd be sisters-in-law," Carla sighed happily. "Wouldn't that be great? You could move back to Frazier Falls, and people wouldn't be able to accuse me of being friendless anymore."

"As if I'd move back here. I love New York. Besides, how'd you end up friendless here? You were one of the boys."

Carla made a face. "Most of the guys who are still here got married, and their wives didn't like them hanging out with me."

Though I'd been Carla's only close female friend, she'd

still been pretty friendly with girls who were deemed unpopular by the in-crowd. I felt a twinge of guilt that I had abandoned my friendship with her—even if only for a few months—for such shallow people.

"Damn." Nick whistled. "Now there's a guy I could get into—" He stared toward the middle Cooper brother who had just arrived with Rich.

"Nick," I warned. "Eli belongs to Emily." I turned him to face Rich. "That one may be up your alley. No one knows."

He lifted his eyes and smiled. "Well, now, I can't deny we'd make the most beautiful pair."

The group laughed raucously as they stared at Carla's brother, Rich. I wondered how he would react if he heard the conversation. Would he be offended or encouraged? The jury was still out on Rich's sexuality, but I knew Nick was as good as Sherlock and would pursue every lead until he got to the bottom of the mystery.

"Speaking of Eli, didn't he punch someone because of you, Carl?" Lauren, the girl from high school, asked.

Carla shook her head. "You have it the wrong way around. Bobby Flynn punched Eli. I heard about it a few months ago—apparently, Pax told Bobby I'd never liked him and thought he was disgusting or something. Bobby got mad and threatened Pax, but Eli stepped in and took the hit."

"Not his smartest moment. Does that man know when to quit?" Lauren asked.

"I'm pretty sure he does. Only now he tosses words and not punches," Carla answered.

Lauren continued, "But Eli did punch someone, didn't he? Who was it?"

Carla chuckled. "Brady Huck."

I stiffened immediately. I couldn't believe I'd forgotten about that.

"Eli got suspended for three days," I added on quietly.

Everyone looked at me, surprised.

"Yeah, he did," Carla said thoughtfully. "Brady probably had it coming."

"Yeah, Eli was hardly going to put up with the guy who bullied his little brother, was he?"

"I still can't believe that happened. When you look at Paxton now ... God. Can't imagine anyone being capable of bullying him. He's so dreamy," Lauren said.

My face warmed uncomfortably. I wasn't so ignorant that I didn't know I was jealous.

Nick laughed when he saw me.

"You're so transparent, Rosie," he whispered for only me to hear. "You're the one he's sleeping with, right? Who cares what these women say?"

"It won't stop them fawning over him at the wedding." I hated the idea of Paxton being bombarded by women at the ceremony, leaving me with no time alone with him. I hated it even more because I knew it was an inevitability.

Lauren and Melanie glanced at each other, then me.

"What?"

"Brady confessed his love for you when you were a sophomore."

"Love is pushing it, but he did like me," I replied uncomfortably. It wasn't something I ever dwelled on. I had almost forgotten it.

Carla looked at the other girls in surprise. "He did?"

"He was obsessed with her," Lauren said. "I shared a few classes with the two of you, and he was always looking at you like you were his next meal. It was creepy."

"I'm pretty sure he stalked you at one point," Melanie added.

My face grew pale. "I didn't know that." Brady was strange, but to stalk me was something entirely different.

Carla grew concerned. "Let's not talk about stalking, that

is scary. I won't be going back to Huck's bar, even if his dad's a sweetheart."

But the women continued their story. "When he confessed his undying love to you, didn't you say you had your heart set on Paxton?"

"I—what?"

Lauren nodded as Melanie said, "Yeah, your locker was by mine, so I heard the whole thing. You told Brady you were in love with Paxton. I always thought it was strange because you didn't even talk to the poor guy."

Oh, holy hell. "Obviously, I didn't mean it," I mumbled, embarrassed, "I wanted Brady to leave me alone."

"Why didn't you just say no, that you didn't like him? Why lie?"

"Because ... he wasn't taking no for an answer." The memory suddenly came back to me. Him pinning me against the locker and telling me I was his. I told him I could never be because my heart belonged to Paxton.

The two women looked at me with frowns on their faces. "You're to blame for all his torment. Saying what you did put a huge target on his back."

My hands fisted, and I was certain the pressure would shatter the glass. Who were these women to judge me? They didn't know me. I struggled to keep my voice level. "Why would you say that?"

Lauren looked at me in disbelief. "Because it's the truth. You were so self-involved you didn't consider the consequences of throwing Paxton under the bus."

Carla stepped forward as if she meant to stop the conversation. "Look, let's not ruin tonight by talking about an obviously sore subject. This happened years ago, so who cares? Now that the boys are arriving, let's give them their space and go to The Bobbly Olive for a few cocktails."

I glanced over my shoulder at John and that woman

Paxton had been talking to at the cocktail party two weeks ago—Ruthie. The pair of them were watching us, with faces that screamed *If a fight is imminent, take it outside.*

"Fine," I said, making for the door. "Since this is obviously so important, let's talk outside."

"I mean, that's not what I meant …" Carla mumbled as the group paid their tab and left Reilly's.

Nick linked arms with me. "What's going on?" he asked.

"Hell if I know."

I turned to face the two women as we made our way to The Bobbly Olive.

"What's your problem with me? What did I ever do to you for you to have such a low opinion of me?"

Melanie rolled her eyes. "It's not as if you ever did anything to us. Besides, we'd have wanted nothing to do with you after what happened to Paxton."

I rephrased my question. "Tell me what happened to Paxton, or I swear to God I'll slap it out of you."

Lauren's face darkened. Out of the corner of my eye, I saw Carla nervously run a hand through her hair, as if she knew the night was about to change.

"You know what, Rose, when you act like this, I can totally see why you and Brady would have been perfect for each other," Lauren said. "You're both bullies."

"What are you talking about?" I all but roared, furious and confused.

"Paxton," Melanie yelled in answer. "Brady went after him because of you. I can't believe the poor guy had to go through all that bullshit he did because you blurted out his name in your little ruse."

"What?"

It was the question I'd been about to ask, but I hadn't gotten the word out.

It was Paxton who spoke.

CHAPTER NINETEEN

PAXTON

It was inevitable that we were going to come across the women during their bachelorette party. This was Frazier Falls, and there were only so many places to go.

I'd expected I'd hear a lot of outrageous stories from both Owen's and Carla's years at high school throughout the evening. I hadn't expected to hear something that changed my entire outlook on my high school life.

"Paxton." A woman I vaguely remembered was shouting to the group of women on the sidewalk. We had gotten into earshot of them on our way to Reilly's.

The entire bachelor party immediately perked up to listen when they heard my name spoken so loudly.

"Brady went after him because of you," the woman continued.

What was she talking about? Any mention of Brady put me on edge.

"I can't believe the poor guy had to go through all that bullshit he did because you blurted out his name in your little ruse."

I froze. Brady had made my life a living hell for Rose?

"What?" I heard myself ask out loud as the two wedding parties came together on the street. I located Rose almost immediately. She seemed as immobile as I was.

The woman who'd spoken flinched when she saw me.

"Paxton, I didn't realize you guys were around the corner from us. I—"

"What are you talking about?" I demanded. "Brady went … Brady did everything he did because of Rose?"

Rose's eyes were wide like she'd seen a ghost. "Paxton, it isn't like that."

"Then what was it like? Because it sounds an awful lot like Brady Huck started bullying me because of you."

The woman who'd spoken in the first place shifted uncomfortably. "That's because it's true," she explained. "Rose said she couldn't go out with him because of you, so he went after you."

Rose looked at the woman in outrage. "That was not what happened." She took a few steps toward me, but I backed away. "Paxton, that's not what—"

"Brady told you he liked you, and you used me?"

"Yes, but—"

"You used me as an excuse to, what? Not go out with him? Or…"

Or maybe she'd said it knowing Brady would start bothering me.

She stared at me as if she knew the conclusion I'd reached. "It's not what you're thinking. Listen to me. Why would I even do that? Why would—"

I put my hand up to stop her from talking. I needed to think. I needed to—I didn't know what I needed.

It certainly wasn't Rose trying to get out of something else that was clearly her responsibility. If what I went through was her fault, it was unforgivable.

"Do you know what I had to go through because of him?"

Not caring that there were close to twenty people standing on the sidewalk listening to what I said, I decided it was time to come clean.

Owen stared at me. Eli looked on with his lips pursed as if this entire confrontation was a long time coming, and he had no intention of stopping it. Carla and Rich and Emily looked on as if they were half a second away from stepping in to try and calm everything down.

Rose looked at me with guilt-ridden eyes, which was all I needed to see.

"He convinced two of my teachers that I'd been cheating on my mid-terms, so I failed." My voice was quiet, but it grew louder as I continued. "He stole my bag every other day, and I'd find it, dripping wet, in my locker when it was time to go home. He hung me upside-down from the bleachers." My voice grew louder. "He threw me in the creek in the middle of winter, keeping my head below the surface until I was certain I would drown. He threatened to cut my tongue out, knife in hand, since I wasn't using it anyway. He—"

"Paxton, stop," Rose cried as she tried to close the distance between us. "I had no idea Brady ever went so far."

"That's the only reason you feel bad? Because you never knew he'd go so far? Did you want him to bully me, so I knew my place? So you could make my life a misery?"

"That's not what I'm saying. I didn't know. This wasn't because of me."

"Yes, he did all of that because of you!" I roared. "I went through hell because of you. God, I was so stupid."

All around, people stared. If the roles were reversed, I'd definitely be staring, but the looks of pity on everyone's faces were unbearable, especially my brothers.

Owen looked stricken. He had no clue any of this had ever gone on.

Even Eli was pale. I'd never told him the specifics of what

Brady had done to me. I had inferred it was terrible, but I imagine hearing exactly what the man had done back in high school shed a new light on everything.

"Brady did all of that?" a voice in the crowd murmured. "Geez."

"Rose got him to, and that makes it worse." Melanie pointed at her.

"I didn't," she protested. She looked like a rabbit trapped by a fox. "I didn't know."

"You obviously wanted something to happen to Paxton," Lauren said. "Otherwise, why would you have brought him up to Brady in the first place? Why Paxton of all people? He was easy prey."

"Didn't Rose bully Paxton back in middle school?" someone added on.

"I thought it was elementary school," another voiced.

"How many years have passed, and it's still going on? That's ridiculous," Emily grumbled.

"I didn't—it wasn't— Paxton, let me talk to you in private," Rose begged, trying to grab on to my sleeve.

I pulled away from her. "Don't touch me. All this time, it was you. It always goes back to you. Always."

"Paxton —"

"No."

Unable to cope with the people watching me, I turned and walked away.

I never wanted to look at or touch or listen to Rose again. I was done.

"Paxton, wait up," Eli called out as he ran after me.

I didn't slow down, but eventually, he reached my side.

Neither of us said anything until we were well away from the group. All I wanted was a bottle of whiskey and my bed.

When we reached my front door, he stopped me. "Wait, let's talk about this."

"What is there to talk about? Rose turned Brady loose on me. I went through hell for her amusement. Years of relentless torture."

He shook his head. "I'm not sure about that."

"You doubt anything we heard?"

"No, but I don't think that kind of malicious bullying is Rose's thing."

"Oh, so you're suddenly on her side?"

"Paxton, shut the hell up."

Eli's lips stretched into a thin line. He was more of the stand back and judge guy, not the step up and fight guy unless it came to me.

"I'm not coming to her defense, but the two of you seemed to have talked over everything Rose did to you in the past and made peace with it. As much as it pains me to say it, I like her."

"You *like* her?"

"Let me finish. You think she would deliberately set Brady on you? She seemed to be as shocked as you were by the accusation."

"She's only affected because she got caught," I spat. "She had me believing she'd changed, that she was sorry. She had me…" *She has me falling in love with her.*

"Pax, I'm the most cynical person you'll ever meet, and I don't believe she acted with malice. Not then, and not now."

I opened my front door. "People don't change. Rose would have had me believe she was never part of what happened. She'd have told me about it if it were innocent. She could have made fun of me over it, but she didn't. She kept silent because she didn't want me to know."

"Maybe she didn't know."

I laughed. The sound was hideously sinister. "I highly doubt that. You were right all along to not like her. Congratulations on being the only one to see through her act."

"Pax—"

I slammed the door.

Grabbing a half-full bottle of whiskey from my kitchen, I collapsed onto my bed and swallowed copious amounts.

I couldn't believe this was happening to me. Would I have been content with carrying on things with Rose the way they'd been going, blissfully unaware of the hand she had in my hell of a life?

I took another swig. Only a fool chose ignorance. It was better to know. Better to steer clear of a woman who'd never had my best interests at heart.

In my pocket, my cell phone buzzed incessantly. I pulled it out, tempted to launch it across my room to watch it smash to pieces. Instead, I unlocked it to see who was trying to contact me.

Almost everyone I knew, it seemed.

I'd missed calls from Owen, concerned messages from Carla and Emily and Rich, stupid social media updates alluding to drama occurring at the bachelor and bachelorette parties.

No message from Rose. I didn't know why I expected there to be. Maybe so she could continue groveling for forgiveness while she maintained her innocence.

She knew it had gone too far. There was nothing she could say to change my mind. I thought about the last two and a half weeks, and how so much had changed between the two of us, but nothing had really changed.

Rose was still toying with me like I was a plaything instead of a person. Better to know what she was truly like rather than miss her when she was gone.

Even the notion of getting to a point where I would miss her put me on edge. She had completely messed with my head. And my heart, though I hated to admit it.

Swigging more whiskey, I leaned back in bed and closed my eyes, begging for my thoughts of her to become vacant.

Damn if she didn't stay there. Wouldn't go away. Everything she'd done, everything she'd said and hadn't.

The apology was only given because she wanted something from me. She was bored and in Frazier Falls. She wanted attention. Never once had she said she cared for me because this was all one of her games.

My thoughts grew darker and darker as every memory the two of us had made over the past couple of weeks became sullied. Part of me didn't want to do this. Part of me wanted to keep the memories the way they were. I'd enjoyed myself, so why couldn't I keep that good feeling?

A larger part of me wanted all the recollections to burn, to forget about her the same way she had forgotten that she'd played a fundamental part in my miserable existence.

Yet, Owen and Carla's wedding was fast approaching, and I'd have to get through it, pretending everything was hunky-dory for them. I'd look at Rose and smile and feign happiness despite the bile boiling in my gut. It was more than I could bear.

She hadn't ruined things that had happened in the past. That was already a done deal. She was so corrupt she was ruining things for me that hadn't yet occurred.

CHAPTER TWENTY

ROSE

When I realized James Rivers had never cared for me—how he could so easily throw our entire relationship in my face to get with some unknown woman in a bar in front of me—I hadn't thought I could be more miserable than that. I was so wrong.

Sitting in Alice's Diner, mindlessly playing around with the bacon and eggs on my plate, I'd never felt worse in my life. The way I'd felt after the betrayal was nothing compared to knowing Paxton believed me to be responsible for the hell he went through in high school—a time that influenced the rest of his life.

It was only made worse by his admission of how bad it had been. I didn't think Eli had known the extent of the problem if his expression was an indicator. Neither had Owen, let alone everyone else who had been there when Paxton lost it. No one had known anything, which meant he had suffered in silence.

The worst part was whether I'd known it or not, it was my fault. Idiotic, brutish, immature, and jealous Brady Huck had tormented him because of me. Had I merely rejected the guy straight out, this would have never happened, but I'd used Paxton's name because the truth was, I'd always loved him. No matter how much I tried to bury the reality, it was there. When I told Brady I had a thing for Paxton, it was the truth my heart already knew.

My phone vibrated with the notification of a new message every so often. Sometimes it was Carla. Other times, Nick. Once, it had been Emily. None of the messages were from Paxton. Why would they be? I'd completely humiliated him.

Tears stung my eyes, threatening to well up and fall at any given moment.

Crying in the diner two days before Carla's wedding was not how I saw this trip going. It didn't help that I also wanted to cry on Paxton's behalf, now that I knew how badly he'd been tortured.

I jumped when my phone rang. Sighing, I answered the call from my mom. There was no way she'd let me get away with ignoring her.

"Rose." Her voice was angry parent serious. The last time I heard this kind of sternness was the day she caught me sneaking back into the house after I TP'd my English teacher's house for giving me a B on a test. "What is this I'm hearing about you and Brady Huck?"

"It's not what it seems, Mom."

"Something in the tone of your voice suggests it's not entirely untrue, either."

"That would be correct."

"Rosie, what's going on? Did you really pick on Paxton all through school? I thought we'd stopped all that princess stuff."

I paused for a moment. "Up until we entered high school … yeah," I admitted. "Nothing bad. Name-calling. Insulting him. That kind of thing."

"Rose, I did not raise you to—"

"I know, Mom." I bit out. "I know you didn't. But I stopped, okay? I stopped before high school. I don't understand why we have to rehash it. Over the past couple of weeks, I've been making it up to him. I apologized. We were getting along with each other. Everything was going great."

My mom sighed. "What's all this about Brady Huck?"

I sniffed, feeling tears fill my eyes once more. "It's not the way you heard it. Not at all. But it's still my fault."

"What happened?"

I took a shaky breath. "When I was a sophomore, Brady Huck told me he liked me. He asked me out. I told him no, but he was insistent. Told me I should give him a shot. I may have told him I was in love with Paxton."

"Rose."

"I know, I know. Back then, I didn't know why I said his name," I shrugged. "Or maybe my head and heart were in sync for once. Paxton was the guy least likely to refute what I said because he never spoke. I thought that was the end of it. When Brady started bullying Paxton, I honestly had no idea it was because of me. How could I have known, Mom?"

My mother paused. "Honey, did you tell Paxton this?"

I shook my head. "I tried to, but there were so many people there, and everyone ganged up on me. It only became a topic of conversation because of Lauren and Melanie. Once Paxton showed up, things got worse."

"Is this Lauren MacMillan and Melanie Jones? Tina's and Briony's girls?"

"Yep."

"I'll be having words with their mothers. Nobody slanders my little girl and gets away with it."

"Mom, I appreciate the gesture, but it's okay. I'll handle it. I'm an adult, and I'd never be able to face myself if I couldn't sort out my problems."

"Even so, what they did was unacceptable. There's the wedding and the whole town is talking. We need to make sure everyone knows the truth."

I choked out a laugh that sounded far more like I was crying. "I'm pretty sure we're well past that. Look, I'll put on a brave face for Carla, but once the ceremony is over, I'll get an early flight back to New York."

"You will not," a male voice behind me suddenly said. For one long, drawn-out moment, I was convinced it was Paxton until I turned and saw Eli.

"Um, Mom, I'll call you back." I hung up as Eli slid into the seat opposite me.

He looked at my plate. "You gonna eat this?"

I shook my head.

"No? Great." He pulled the plate toward him and wolfed down my untouched breakfast.

"Why are you here, Eli?"

He looked at my plate pointedly. "For the free food. It was by sheer chance I overheard your conversation with your mom."

I frowned. "How much did you hear?"

"All of it."

"So, you stood behind me for the better part of ten minutes without making it known you were there?"

"Yes. Do you have a problem with that?"

I slumped against my seat. "Not really. Be careful, you're in the presence of Frazier Falls' most hated woman. What would Emily say?"

"She'd tell you to line up behind her so cut the crap, Rogers. We both know you're not as bad as all that."

"You've never been a fan."

"I don't hate you. I dislike you and with good reason. You ignored Carl in school and needlessly picked on Paxton."

"I ... yeah. Whatever. That's all true. Not much of a difference between dislike and hate, though, is there?"

He looked up at me seriously. "There's all the difference in the world."

"Huh?"

He stole my glass of water in order to wash down the food. "Dislike I can get over. Dislike can change if I see the person making an effort to make up for their past mistakes. Dislike can be thrown to the side if I see my brother falling in love with you only to have his heart ripped to pieces by mindless slander"

I flinched at the comment about Paxton falling in love with me. It hurt too much. I gulped softly. "And hate?"

"If you honestly had a hand in what Brady did to Paxton, I wouldn't be here. And I'd make sure everyone knew how despicable you are. That's my gift."

I bristled at the threat. "Good thing I didn't do it, then."

He smiled lopsidedly. "Exactly."

"But what can I do? The way he reacted last night; I don't think anything I say will get through to him. He was devastated."

"That's because he's never dealt with what Brady did to him. Although, hearing him talk about it, I can see why. The son of a bitch is lucky he got away with me merely punching him."

"That isn't helping."

"I know, but it feels damn good to think about exacting revenge."

I sat up suddenly, a stupid idea having occurred to me. "Revenge doesn't need to be in the past," I murmured.

He grinned wickedly. "I like your train of thought, Rogers. I somehow doubt I could get Owen to help me out with something this immature, but you could."

"You've got that right."

I thought about retaliation on Brady. Not only for Paxton but for myself. He'd used me as an excuse to hurt a person I cared about more than most anyone else. People think we outgrow our childhood hurts, but they are what mold us into the people we are. Those wounds never heal.

"Do you have any ideas in mind? I'd love to hear them." Love to make Brady pay for what he did to both Paxton and me.

He shrugged. "A few. Several of them would get us arrested, so they're out because Emily doesn't like to sleep alone. Let me think on it today, and we can do something about the asshole tomorrow."

"Thank you."

He glanced at me. "For what?"

"For believing me when you absolutely didn't need to. I don't deserve your support."

He laughed lightly. "Paxton doesn't deserve to get his heart ripped in two, but I guess you don't deserve being hated by everyone, either. You're not all bad."

"That sounded almost heartfelt."

"Rosie."

I froze. Staring at Eli's confused face, I desperately tried to resist the urge to turn around to deal with the man whose voice echoed through my head. In the end, I caved and looked.

"James, what are you doing in Frazier Falls?" There wasn't an ounce of friendliness in my voice.

He smiled brilliantly when he realized I wasn't going to ignore him. "Rosie, I'm so glad to see you. I've been trying to get in contact with you. I went to your office so many times."

"What do you want?"

He came around to stand at the front of the booth Eli and I were sitting at, blocking any means of escape. He ignored Eli as if he didn't exist.

"Rose, I want you back. I miss you so much. I made such a huge, terrible mistake."

"You didn't seem to think so when you were kissing that woman's face off at the bar. You told me we were never exclusive."

Those last few sentences I spoke loudly, ensuring everybody in the diner could hear them.

He squirmed uncomfortably. "Rose, can we talk about this in private?"

"Come on, James, you're not really the private kind of guy or the exclusive kind either."

"Please, Rose, we're good together. You look good on my arm and on my bio. I'm good for yours too. We're a power couple."

How could I have ever thought I was in love with him? It was clear to me now that I'd only ever been a trophy. The girlfriend his parents approved of, and his boss liked. I was the woman he was supposed to have, not the one he wanted to have. Two weeks ago, I would have accepted a merger, but now, I wanted more and needed more.

Eli cleared his throat. "I'm sorry, but could you stop harassing my girlfriend?" His voice was full of false politeness. He gave my leg a subtle kick under the table as if to tell me to play along.

James looked at Eli in shock. "Rosie? You're already with someone else?"

"An old high school flame." Eli beamed. "We couldn't keep our hands off each other when we reunited again. Isn't that right, Rosie?"

I struggled so hard to keep from laughing but nodded my head. "When I saw him, I realized I'd never not been in love with him. Thank you for setting me free and showing me what I truly wanted." While the whole thing was a ruse, the words were true. He had set me free, which allowed me to see the truth. Paxton was my one that got away.

James looked like he'd been slapped. He seemed to grapple with his temper for a few moments. "When you get back to New York, you'll realize you made a mistake."

I stared at him coldly. "Yes, you're right, you were a mistake."

"Time to leave, buddy," Eli said mildly before turning back to me as if our conversation had never been interrupted. "So, about our plans for tomorrow."

It took another minute or two, but James eventually got the picture. He stormed out red-faced and humiliated. As soon as he was out of earshot, I burst into laughter.

"Oh my, you wonderful, wonderful man. Thank you."

Eli laughed as hard as I did. "I did it as much for my own amusement as anything else. He's a real piece of work, huh?"

"I don't know what I ever saw in him."

"Hard to say. Paycheck? His sense of fashion? Puts you to sleep? Love is weird that way."

"There was no love. Only..." I was going to say sex, but even that wasn't mention-worthy. "Not that either."

"Awful."

"Yep, and it makes me wonder if Carla and Owen hadn't been getting married if Paxton and I would have started speaking again?"

He rolled his eyes. "Who cares about ifs? You did. And it was good for the two of you. Leave it at that, and let's fix the mess we have in front of us."

I held my hand up in mock-salute. "Roger that, Cooper."

"Please tell me you don't use your surname like that on a regular basis."

"Only when I don't care what people will think of me."

"So ... never, then?"

"Rude."

He moved out of his seat and came around to my side of the booth. When he nudged me to move over and give him room, I looked at him questioningly.

"What are you doing?"

He kissed my cheek, and there was a clicking sound, and then he moved back to his own seat.

"Taking a memento of our long-awaited bonding," he joked as he inspected the photo he had snapped with his cell phone. "Plus, I'm sure Paxton would love to see it."

I winced. "You honestly think he could ever forgive me?"

"You'll never know if all you do is sit there worrying about it. Let's do something instead." He tucked his phone back inside his pocket. "Don't let Emily know I claimed you as my girlfriend. She'll shank you after she castrates me."

I couldn't believe I'd never known this side of Eli before. He was going out of his way to help me, even though he could as easily have left things the way they were.

"Deal. I've already had the public hanging. I'll pass on the impaling."

CHAPTER TWENTY-ONE

PAXTON

Though I had been dreading building Owen and Carla's damn floating wedding stage, I found myself now glad for the work. It was methodical and distracting and solitary.

It was exactly what I needed to work out my anger at Rose.

No. Anger didn't cover how I felt about her. Not in the slightest. What she had done to me warranted far more than anger. I was hurt, and that was worse. The pain I felt was unimaginable. That was something I could never forgive.

A sharp whack of the hammer in my hand caused me to immediately recoil. I'd hit my thumb, and it was now angry and red.

"For the love of Pete," I muttered, rubbing away at the affected skin until the pain subsided. Now I'd likely have a bruised hand to go along with my ego.

It was another thing I could blame her for.

"Paxton."

I turned my head, scowling when I saw both Owen and Eli walking toward me.

"This is looking great," Owen said. "I knew you were the

right person for the job. Seems like you'll have it finished early. Carla will be thrilled."

I balked at the idea of finishing the physical work early. I needed it to distract me right up until the moment I had to complete it.

I didn't respond to Owen's compliments, instead choosing to turn back to concentrate on the stage, but I'd already forgotten which part I'd been working on. I dropped my hammer and sat up, wiping dirt and sweat away from my forehead.

"I take it you're both here to talk about what happened the other night," I responded flatly.

"Obviously," Eli replied as the two of them sat down on the bank of the creek.

We were silent for a few moments, and I wondered if they were waiting for me to speak first.

Eventually, Owen said, "Why didn't you tell me about Brady, Pax? Clearly, Eli knew some of it but not all of it."

I grimaced. "What would you have done about it? You started working as an architect in New York. And Eli couldn't keep protecting me. His interference only made the problems worse."

"I'd have come back and helped you deal with it," Owen exclaimed.

Eli held a hand up to calm him down. "I get if you felt that you wanted to deal with him yourself, or that you didn't want to bother us, but Pax, what he did was serious. The least you could have done was tell Mom and Dad."

"And then what? Come on, Eli. Give me some credit. I graduated high school and went to college and sorted myself out. We all have to grow up and take care of our own shit. The shit with Brady didn't affect me as badly as you seem to think it had."

They looked at me in disbelief. "You're calling the other night not affecting you badly?"

I looked away. "I'd been dealing with it fine until then. It honestly wasn't something I thought about much."

Owen frowned. "Did you never ask him at the time why he was bullying you?"

"What part of silence was my sword do you keep forgetting?" I fired back. "I couldn't find the words to tell our parents. Half the time when he was bullying me to my face, he had my head underwater, or my airway blocked. At which point was I supposed to up and ask him, 'Hey, why are you doing this?' and expect him to answer?"

Owen and Eli shifted uncomfortably. Clearly, the two of them realized I was correct, but they didn't want to admit to it.

There was another minute or two of silence before Owen said, "Rose wasn't responsible for Brady. You have to know that."

"I don't want to talk about her," I muttered, turning from the two of them.

"Is that why the stuff with Brady is bothering you so much?" Eli asked. "Because of what Melanie Jones said about it being Rose's fault?"

"It's irrelevant. I'm just angry."

"Because you can't deal with thinking she'd been messing with you the entire time, and that everything that's happened over the past couple of weeks has been a lie?"

"Whatever."

"Stop being so ridiculous," Owen spat out. "You saw how she reacted that night with your own eyes. Don't you dare say it's because she hadn't expected to get caught. She was heartbroken to think she might have been the reason you were terrorized."

"She didn't know why he was doing it at the time," Eli added on.

"That makes it worse." Angry tears stung my eyes, but I blinked them away. "Even when she had no idea she was doing it, she was there, all the time, tormenting me."

"She was scared of Brady too," Owen said gently. "I asked the girls about it. Lauren MacMillan admitted that Melanie had gone too far in accusing her of being responsible for what happened. I guess she didn't like Rose much. Either way, Lauren told me Rose tried to outright refuse him, but he kept pressuring her and intimidating her. She never got why Rose said she was in love with you when, in reality, she could have said any guy's name on the football team, and they'd have happily dated her as a decoy."

"How is this supposed to make me feel better?" I asked sullenly.

"It's supposed to make you understand. Rose said she loved you because deep inside, I think she did. Besides all of that, Brady was stalking her."

My eyes widened at Eli's statement. "He was what?"

"Rose didn't know it, but Lauren admitted to seeing him following her around school. Caught him lurking outside her house. Rose only found out the other night. I think she was pretty shaken by it, but then the girls started pushing the blame for what happened to you on her."

"She should have called me about it."

"As if you'd have picked up a call from her," Owen scoffed. "If you'd hung around for another five minutes, you'd have been there when Eli and I wheedled the whole truth out of Lauren. But no, you had to run off like a scorned lover."

"What happened to you was awful. Beyond awful. And I still don't understand how you could have kept so quiet about it even taking into account your personality," Eli added on when I raised an eyebrow. "But my point is," he continued, "you can't blame her for it. You're only hurting yourself. Can't you see that?" He shook his head. "It's like damn high school all over again."

"I know she teased you when you were kids," Owen said. "But you'd made up, right? In what world did she deserve the treatment she got?"

"I …"

Owen smiled sympathetically when I didn't finish my sentence. "I know you want to act like you hate her. You want to be able to blame her. You finally found out the reason why Brady attacked you, and it had to do with her. I know that must have stung like a bitch, but that isn't her fault, no matter how you spin it."

I was silent. I didn't know what to say. I'd been ready to act like Rose was dead to me. To pretend she'd never existed, but deep inside, I knew I couldn't let go of Rose because a world with Rose in it was a hundred percent better than a world without her. Here were my brothers, who I trusted more than anyone else, telling me I was wrong—confirming what I knew to be true. I couldn't blame her when it was Brady who delivered the torture.

I burst out laughing.

Eli and Owen looked taken aback.

"What?" Owen asked uncertainly.

"Why are we all so screwed up?" I stared at him. "You don't tell anyone but Eli about your panic attacks, and even then, it was only because he walked in on one. I literally had to see you almost vomit on stage to know what was going on with you." I turned to Eli. "You literally stopped eating and sleeping because of Emily, and you were in complete denial about how much she meant to you. The whole time you didn't say a word to us about it. And me …"

The two of them chuckled.

"Yeah, no need to explain what's wrong with you, you weirdo," Eli said.

We only laughed harder at that.

I wasn't sure what to do about Rose. Not yet. My heart felt too raw and exposed. How was it that a wound in my childhood could fester into the cavernous hole I felt today? It just proved how powerful words were when said in anger. The razor-sharp edge of an accusation could eviscerate. I loved her, but I wasn't sure what to do with that revelation.

For now, I had a wedding stage to complete. Everything else could wait.

I smiled at my brothers. "If you want me to get this finished on time, then I'd suggest you leave me alone."

"You sure you'll be okay? You're not going to jump in the creek and try to drown yourself?"

"Hilarious. Go away. Both of you."

"Peace out," Eli laughed as they walked away.

I turned back to my work, feeling better and worse about myself. It was a bizarre sensation.

No matter what I chose to do about Rose, I knew I could behave myself at the wedding and be civil. That had been what the two of us had wanted from the beginning. Now if I could just figure out the rest of it.

CHAPTER TWENTY-TWO

ROSE

Why was I so nervous? Every breath I took in was shaky and uncertain, as if at any moment, I might turn tail and run right back to New York without another word. But Eli's eyes were on me, telling me not to go. I had to do this. Not for me, but for Paxton.

Rich Stevenson and Nick were with us. Nick, of course, was in on the revenge plot and was on board to help in under a second. Rich had been more surprising when he told us Brady had picked on many people including him. It went a long way in explaining why he might like to see the man get a taste of his own medicine.

The fact that Brady's bullying still affected his victims made me think of everything Paxton had said and hadn't said when I'd first arrived back in Frazier Falls. I underestimated how much impact my words and actions could possibly have had on him.

It was high time for me to do more than apologize to Paxton. No, I had to act.

"Ready, Rose?" Eli asked, glancing at me with a small smile.

I flexed and unflexed my right hand, letting my finger joints crack in an exaggerated manner.

"I didn't get all dressed up for nothing. Let's go."

In truth, I was dressed up. Part of Eli's plan was for me to look as beautiful and irresistible as possible. To that end, I'd put on the backless, deep blue dress I'd worn to Frazier Falls, keeping my hair loose and wavy around my face. My lips were painted my favorite shade of dark red.

"You look like you're about ready to murder someone," Nick joked. "Maybe rein in the vengeful energy."

I rolled my eyes but took a few deep breaths and forced myself to calm down.

I smiled at him. "Better?"

"Much better," Nick said, both Rich and Eli nodding in approval.

"Make sure to lead him on as much as possible," Rich said enthusiastically, "so the punchline is way more satisfying."

I quirked an eyebrow. "Are you saying this for the benefit of the plan or for your own amusement?" Eli put an arm around his future brother-in-law's shoulders as he said so. Rich glanced at his arm with slightly surprised eyes. "Right. Nick, Rich, and I will make our way into the bar first. Don't come in until I text you."

I nodded, then leaned back against the wall as the three men made their way inside. Nobody passed me on the street while I waited, which I was grateful for. I was fairly certain at least half the town hated me right now for what I'd supposedly done to Paxton, and I simply didn't have it in me to correct each and every person glaring at me as I went about my business.

It had been like that the day before, on my way to and from the diner. I hadn't been able to take it, so I'd gone straight home, that way I wouldn't have to see anybody.

Acting like this wasn't like me in the slightest. I had always held my head high and gone about my business, no matter what.

I hoped this worked so things could go back to the way they were before. I had to be able to come back to see my mom on occasion and didn't want the inhabitants of Frazier Falls to continue having such a low opinion of me.

A buzz in my hand alerted me to a text from Eli. I smiled grimly. It was showtime.

Remembering everything I knew from working with models and fashionistas in New York, I sauntered into the bar, glancing around until I spotted Brady cleaning a glass. I deliberately slid my sunglasses off to smile at him as I caught his eye, walking purposefully toward him as he put down the glass.

"Why, if it isn't Rose Rogers," he drawled, leaning over the surface as he took in my whole appearance.

I bent over in a mock bow. "In the flesh. It's been a while, Brady."

"You're telling me." The way he looked at me made me feel equal parts uncomfortable and satisfied. Brady was going to fall for this hook, line, and sinker. "What'll it be, Rogers?"

I flashed another smile. "I came in to find you, but I'll have a vodka and lime juice since you're asking."

He kept his eyes on me as he made the drink. "You back in town for Carl's wedding? Most everyone from our high school days is back for it, it seems."

I nodded. "Are you going?" I knew he wasn't, but he couldn't know that.

He laughed bitterly. "I'm not, actually. I think Carl has a problem with me."

I raised an eyebrow. "Not Owen?"

"Owen's been in here to drink a few times with Eli, so I don't see why he'd have an issue with me."

"He's brothers with Princess Paxton."

Brady burst out laughing. "Man, I forgot you used to call him that. He's never set foot in here. His brother is another story. Doesn't come around often, but he shows up on occasion."

I turned my head and spotted Eli, Nick, and Rich sitting in a booth drinking beer. They were the only ones in the place, which was good because they were the only ones to witness what was going down.

"Didn't Eli punch you in the face in high school?"

He laughed. "It's not an issue anymore."

I put a grimace on my face. "I'm not exactly liked by the Coopers right now, either."

"Oh? Is that so?"

I leaned across the bar to get closer, allowing him to see down the front of my dress. The effect was immediate. His eyes took on a hungry sheen as his lips curled into a predatory smile.

"Apparently, we're co-conspirators."

"I like the sound of that. What did we do?"

"Rumor has it, I set you on Paxton back in high school. Admittedly, I had no clue at the time."

I placed a hand on his arm. He looked at it, then back up at my face.

"You said you were in love with him, so he had to go."

I bit my lip. "You must have known the truth. I mean … it was Paxton."

Eli, Nick, and Rich came up to the bar then.

"Another three beers, please," Eli ordered.

Brady glared at him. "Can't you see I'm busy, Cooper?"

Eli stared at me as if he was only seeing me for the first time. His eyes widened in exaggerated shock. "Oh, if it isn't

Rose. I had no idea I'd ever see you in a scum-bag bar like this one."

"Watch your mouth, Cooper. You're here too," Brady growled. "This is my old man's place."

"Yes, and he'd be ashamed," I said.

Brady turned with his face twisted into a scowl.

"What do you mean, Rose?"

The hand I had on Brady's arm tightened on his sleeve. "Your poor father would be ashamed if he knew what his son did for kicks in high school. More than ashamed, I'd say."

"What the hell are you talking about?" His fist came down on the bar and rattled the dirty glasses he hadn't cleaned.

"I had to hear with my own ears that you attacked Paxton because of me," I cut in. "You knew exactly what you were doing. Not only had you scared me so much that I wanted you to leave me alone, but you put Paxton through hell because I loved him." Saying it out loud was a relief.

I paused, watching Brady carefully as his face warped into something entirely unpleasant. "Were you planning to force me to go out with you after you were done with him?"

"You were always acting like you were too good for me, even now. Like I'm supposed to fall at your feet because you walk into my bar dressed like a fashion queen. You're not better than me."

"That's where you're wrong. I am a hell of a lot better than you. I don't try and drown people in creeks, hang them from the bleachers, and threaten them with knives simply because I can't get someone to date me."

He laughed cruelly. "The freak deserved everything he got. He never even asked me to stop. I bet he got off on it—"

I wound up and punched him in the face.

Brady recoiled in shock, so I vaulted over the bar and punched him again, so hard that he ended up on the floor. Looking down, I realized my dress had risen too high on my thighs, so I yanked it down because, after all, I was a lady, and ladies didn't show their goodies to just anyone.

"Holy shit," I heard Nick murmur. "Didn't know you could do that, Rose."

"Looks like those self-defense classes in college came in handy." I stared down at Brady, "You talk like that about Paxton again, and I swear to God you're going to get more than a punch to the face."

"What, so now he has a girl fighting his battles for him?" Brady spat on the floor. "How noble."

"No, this is for me," I said. "But the three guys over there might have something to say or do on his behalf."

I stabbed a stilettoed foot into the floor close to his groin, and the sound was like a gunshot. He winced away.

Eli laughed. "I think you're making our point clear, Rogers. You might want to smile. You're on camera."

Brady swung his head around wildly to look up at Eli, whose cell phone was pointed in our direction.

"You son of a—"

"I'm sure your dad would love to see this."

"Don't you dare—"

"He'd probably take this place away from you. Can't have a lowbrow bully like you running his business, can he?"

Brady sucked in a rattling breath. He knew, perfectly well, his father would take the bar away. Whether he admitted it out loud or not, it was all Brady had.

"What do you want?" he asked through gritted teeth.

I grinned. "Nothing."

"What?"

"Rose is right," Eli said. "We want absolutely nothing from you. You'll have to trust we'll keep this to ourselves. Don't give us a reason to share it."

I walked around the bar to join Eli, Rich, and Nick. "I'd say he's gotten the message, wouldn't you?"

Brady scowled, too furious to speak—or too afraid. It was hard to tell. I shifted my hand slightly in his direction and was satisfied to see him flinch away.

"Come on, guys," I said. "Let's go."

When we were outside, I was bombarded by hugs from everyone else.

"That was some right hook, Rose." Rich patted me on the back.

"I never knew you had that in you," Nick said.

"I could almost fall for you," Eli growled. "I like my women spirited."

I laughed at his remark. "Don't forget that Emily has knife skills."

"That girl has all sorts of talents." He whistled.

I was quiet for a moment too long.

Rich cocked his head. "You're going to make up with Paxton, right?"

"After all of this, you have to," Nick added.

I looked at Eli, begging him to understand.

"I can't. I have to leave him alone. It was what he always wanted. I finally understand that it's not a challenge for me to try and overturn. I need to be the bigger person and let him live his life without me in it."

Eli nodded in understanding. "You say that just as I'm beginning to like you?"

I made like I would punch him on the arm, but he retreated.

"Hey, you're not touching me after what I saw you do to Brady."

Laughter bubbled up inside me. "Fair enough."

"What are you going to do now?" Rich asked. "You want to come by and stay with Carl and me?"

I shook my head, grabbing Nick as I did.

"I think I'll be fine. I have my best friend, and a mom

who's probably feeling neglected."

Nick grinned at me. "Look at you, all grown up."

I rolled my eyes. "Shut up."

But it was true. It felt like I'd matured, which made what I felt for Paxton hurt all the more.

CHAPTER TWENTY-THREE

PAXTON

The fact that the wedding was tomorrow hadn't quite sunk in yet. The stage was finished, but I pretended it wasn't so people would leave me alone. I knew it was selfish. There was so much to be set up, but I didn't have it in me to care.

How could I be excited for a wedding, considering everything that had happened? Even as I told myself it wasn't fair to act this way—that I could still be happy for Owen and Carla even as my heart was stinging—I couldn't stop myself from spiraling inside my head. Even after everything Owen and Eli had said to me to try and clear it, I still felt miserable.

"Paxton."

Speak of the devil. I gritted my teeth and kept my back turned away from him. I knew he was likely here to make me feel better or talk more sense into me.

"Pax, come on," he continued when I ignored him. "What's up?"

"He speaks. I was beginning to forget what your voice sounded like. Felt like high school all over again."

"Hilarious."

He came over and collapsed on the stage.

"Get off. It's not finished yet."

"Hell yes, it's finished. It's been finished for hours, and everyone knows it. They're giving you space, but I'm done with that."

I lie back on the hard wood.

"You're right. I've been avoiding everyone."

Eli held a hand up to his ear as if he hadn't heard me. "What was that? It sounded like you said I was right."

I threw a screw at him that he smoothly avoided.

"I'm sorry. I shouldn't have run off the way I did in the first place when all you were trying to do was talk some sense into me, but I didn't want to listen. Something I usually excel at."

Eli sighed as he moved over to sit beside me. "You need to see something."

When he pulled out his cell phone, I swung back into a sitting position. "What is it?"

"Watch. Don't say anything until the end."

When he started playing a video, I looked closely at his screen, bristling when I realized who the people in the video were.

Rose and Brady.

I glared at him. "What the—"

"Shh," he reprimanded. "Watch. And listen."

I did. I watched as Rose, dressed in that beautiful blue dress of hers, flirted outrageously with a pleased-looking Brady. I couldn't stand the way he looked at her.

"I don't understand why you'd want me to—"

"Shut up and watch."

I turned back to the video as the viewpoint changed. Eli, Rich, and a man I only knew from photos to be Rose's friend Nick had moved to the bar. Brady told them to go away, but then—

DEFEND ME

The conversation turned. Rose scolded Brady for what he'd done to me, and when he said I'd had it coming, she punched him in the face, then she climbed over the bar and punched him again until Brady was on the floor.

I watched the rest of the video in bewilderment as Eli and Rose took turns to drill home if Brady didn't want to lose the bar, he'd do well to never harass anyone again. The look on his face when he realized Eli filmed the entire thing was priceless.

When the video was finished, I looked at him. "When did this happen?"

"About two hours ago."

"Wait, so … when did you decide to do this?"

My brother grinned. "Yesterday. With Rose. I was going to do something about Brady after everything you said regardless, but when I overheard her talking to her mom on the phone, I knew I had to get her to help me."

I frowned. "What was she saying to her mom?"

He shrugged. "The truth. When I heard her admit to her mom that she had teased you as a kid, I knew I could trust her when she said she had no idea why Brady was bullying you. Not that I ever expected her to have known like I said the other night."

"You're so insightful, thanks for rubbing it in." I cast my gaze down. "I should have let her explain herself. I got too caught up in what everyone was saying. It was like going back to high school all over again."

"It would have happened to any of us." He patted me on the back. "It didn't help that she was so upset she could barely get a sentence out."

"That makes it worse."

Eli chuckled. "I guess it does. I thought I'd be happy to see her upset and humiliated by everyone, but it turned out I hated it. She didn't deserve it, especially since the two of you had already made peace with your past."

"I know."

"So why haven't you called her to apologize? Fair enough procrastinating on everything else but to put off Rose? If I hadn't found her in the diner and persuaded her to help me out, she had every intention of getting an early flight back to New York. You wouldn't have had an opportunity to speak to her face to face."

I froze. "She was going to leave before the wedding?"

"She wouldn't miss the actual wedding. She's one of Carla's bridesmaids, but she was going to leave straight after without going to the reception. If you'd been relying on getting some courage in the form of alcohol in order to speak to her, you'd have lost the chance."

"What can I say to her?"

"Did you see her in the video I showed you? She's worked through the upset and moved straight through anger to reach acceptance. She told me she didn't plan on contacting you again to respect your wish for her to leave you alone. Talk about maturity."

"She doesn't plan on speaking to me at the wedding?"

"Now you're getting it. You've got to speak to her first if you want her in your life."

I collapsed back onto the wooden decking, sighing heavily. Eli layed down beside me with a frown.

"I don't like the look on your face right now, Pax," he murmured. "Please tell me you're going to speak to her again. She literally got back at Brady for you. Well, for her too, but that's beside the point. You're clearly crazy about one another, as insane as that still sounds to me."

"I don't know. Maybe it would be better for us if we leave things as they are. She's going back to New York in a few days anyway. What would be the point?"

DEFEND ME

"You're a fool."

I turned to him. "Excuse me?"

He seemed to ignore me, perusing through photos on his cell phone until I glanced at one over his shoulder. "Why the hell are you kissing Rose when you've got Emily?" I was immediately furious.

He grinned, holding his phone closer to me so I could see the photo better. "Doesn't sound like someone who wants to give her up. This was my reward for helping her with her ex-boyfriend."

"Wait, what? When?"

He stretched out like a cat, making a contented noise as he did so. "Yesterday. He rolled into Frazier Falls, begging for her to take him back. Turns out, she caught him cheating on her, and he acted like it was nothing. It's why she came home so early."

"Were they serious?"

He nodded. "Rose thought so. I imagine she was torn up."

A hollow, sick feeling grew in my stomach. I hadn't even asked her why she'd come back early. She must have been in so much pain.

"I can tell what you're thinking from your face, Pax."

"This whole trip was supposed to be a break for her, and I ruined it."

He laughed. "If she wanted you to know, don't you think she would've told you? She was enjoying spending time with you without having anything hanging over her head. The guy treated her like a business deal—a merger of sorts."

I went quiet, considering everything he'd said. Eventually, I asked, "How did you help her get rid of the guy?"

"I pretended to be her new boyfriend."

I choked as I sat up. "You what?"

"Again, evidence that you don't want anyone else to be with her. If you let her go back to New York without telling her how you feel, she's going to run into countless men like her ex and probably a few good guys, too. You want her to be with some unknown New Yorker when she could be with you?"

When I didn't reply, he chuckled.

"You're so transparent. Call her, Pax. Or better yet, head over to her house and apologize to her in person. You can't let this pass you by. You can't let her go."

He was right, which was infuriating because it was Eli, and he loved to be right.

"Thanks," I mumbled.

He pushed me over in response.

"What was that? Was that a 'thank you' I heard from you?"

"You're the worst," I said as I rolled him over so that he was lying face-down on the deck.

"Real mature, Pax," he said with his cheek pressed to the wood. He got up, brushed himself off, and grinned. "You're done here. Let Owen and Carl set up for their big day and go sort your life out. No matter what Rose says, I'll be in Reilly's with Emily having a beer, so feel free to join me if she breaks your heart."

"Such a supportive brother."

"Only the best."

He walked away, leaving me to clean up the tools I'd been pretending to use for the last two hours in a vain attempt to keep busy. It had been so stupid of me to waste my time like that. He was right; Rose could have left, and I'd have lost the opportunity to tell her how I feel.

After I'd cleaned up, I pulled out my phone, not wanting to risk heading to Lucy's house only to find that Rose was out, then I heard footsteps behind me, and I turned to see her smiling.

CHAPTER TWENTY-FOUR

ROSE

"Hey."

It sounded so stupid, so insignificant. After everything that had happened, I chose to say, hey?

I'm an idiot.

Paxton watched me carefully. "I was going to call you."

That was the last thing I'd been expecting.

"You were?"

He nodded, and I took it as a good enough sign to move forward, closing the distance between us. "Paxton, I—"

"It's fine, Rose," he interrupted. "You don't have to say anything."

"But I do, because whether I like it or not, this whole mess was my fault."

"Everything can't be about you, Rose."

I bristled despite myself. "That's unfair." I was here to apologize, not get into another argument. I was only here because Eli insisted that I speak to Paxton before the wedding; otherwise, I wouldn't be here. As recently as five minutes ago, he texted to urge me to speak to his brother, and so here I was.

I had one chance to fix this. I couldn't mess this up.

"Paxton, I never knew why Brady tormented you, but I know why I did."

"You're a sadist?"

The laugh started low in my stomach and moved up like a raging river of hysteria. When I didn't answer, he joined in.

"Sadist? No, but maybe a masochist. I seem to be a magnet for the people who can hurt me the most." Leaning on the rail, I watched the water rush by. It moved by as fast as time. How had fifteen years passed and still the pain of youth scratched at both of us?

"I hurt you?"

"God, yes. Every time you looked at me and didn't say a word. Don't you get it? I liked you then, and I like you now."

"Are you sure you don't want to pull my hair or punch my arm?" He moved closer, closing the gap.

"Oh, I do, but I'd rather kiss you and tell you I think you've turned out to be a wonderful man. More importantly, I want to tell you how sorry I am that you suffered because of my silence."

Paxton took a final step until we were face to face.

"You ... silent?" He shook his head. "The Rose Rogers I know is never without words. Funny you lost your tongue now when there's so much to say, and I've found mine."

"What a mess." I fell forward until my head rested on his chest. The scent of his cologne mixed with sunshine and hard work was the perfect aromatic therapy to ease the strain of a nerve-racking day.

"I'm sorry too. For lots of reasons, but mostly because I of all people know that often what appears to be the truth is not. We all hide behind something. For me, it was silence. For you, I imagine you hid behind a false sense of confidence. We aren't all that different."

I didn't know what to say. Paxton was apologizing to me.

After everything that had happened. Everything I had done. Everything that had transpired. He was apologizing to me.

I looked up at him. "You don't have anything to be sorry for."

He bit out a laugh. "You're not going to let me take responsibility for my own actions?"

I shook my head. "Nope. Taking responsibility for my actions is my new thing."

My face warmed as Paxton brushed his fingers against my cheek.

We were both quiet for a moment; then, I curled my palm around his.

His eyes sparkled with mischief.

"Tell me. How does it feel being the most hated person in Frazier Falls? Well, second-most hated behind Brady. The man has to win at something."

I pulled my hand back so I could slap his chest, but he laughed as he grabbed mine and brought it to his lips for a kiss, his eyes never leaving mine.

"Rose, I'm sorry. Even if you don't want me to say it, it's true."

"Paxton, I—"

"I know you're sorry, too," he interrupted, "for whatever part you played in what Brady did. Even though it was accidental, you were put in a situation where you had to say what you said, and that's terrible. We all say stupid shit out of anger, frustration, or fear."

He pulled me in closer until the only thing between us was our intertwined hands.

"I'm sorry I didn't tell you what I told Brady all those years ago. While I had no idea what love was back then, I never hated you like you thought. I was a kid who had no idea what that messy tangle of feelings meant."

He sighed. "All this time you had a crush on me, Rogers?

Imagine that. Wouldn't it have been easier to say you were in love with someone on the football team? You were dating Reggie at the end of your sophomore year. Shouldn't you have said his name?"

I made a face. "I was never serious about Reggie. I only dated him because of peer pressure. I was a cheerleader, and he was the obvious choice."

He smirked. "Nothing about you is obvious, and here I thought I had you pegged."

"Are you saying I was predictable?"

He tilted my head up with a finger beneath my chin. "You were, but we've both changed, and you're a mystery I'm dead set on solving."

I looked at his handsome face for a few seconds, reveling in the expression that quirked his mouth into a smile and lit up his beautiful blue eyes.

When I closed mine, I threw my arms around his neck and kissed him, as hard and passionately as I could.

He reciprocated, taking a step or two back as I moved against him, our bodies instinctively looking for a vertical surface to lean on. When I opened my eyes, I realized we were on the edge of the wedding stage, the creek flowing below us.

I pulled away and grinned, not giving him a second to compose himself before I pushed him into the water.

I barely heard the sound he made as he crashed into the creek. My laughter rose above the din.

When Paxton surfaced, running a hand over his face to clear away the water, he was laughing, too.

I sat down on the edge of the stage, taking off my shoes to dangle my feet into the stream. He swam over with an impressed look on his face.

"I didn't see that coming," he said.

"Paybacks are hell."

He chuckled. "They sure are. Care to join me?"

I shook my head. "My feet in are enough for me."

He turned his head to look at the other end of the stage, which was secluded by the low-hanging, heavy branches of the trees on the opposite bank of the creek. He smiled wickedly at me.

"What about joining me over there?"

My hand came to my heart as if I were appalled by the claim. "Are you asking what I think you're asking?"

"Depends …" He swam over to the opposite bank, lifting himself onto the stage with strong, tightly-muscled arms before removing his sodden T-shirt. "If what you're thinking of is, us burning off a little excess energy right here and now, then I guess I was asking if you'd be interested."

I laughed as I got to my feet and walked over to meet him. There was no one around, and the trees would do a good job of hiding us. The water would no doubt drown out whatever sounds we made. Before I second-guessed myself, he grabbed me and pulled me beneath him. My clothes absorbed the dripping water, and I pushed away in order to slide my dress up.

"We've got to stop this outside stuff," I joked as he undid the buttons of his pants and pulled them off, throwing them to the side to join his soaked shirt. "It's not a habit I'm inclined to develop."

He chuckled as he grazed his lips against my cheek, planting gentle kisses along my jawline, down my neck, and across my collarbone. He kept the kisses light but sensual. The sensation left me shivering in anticipation.

"We can indulge the habit once more for the sake of christening the wedding stage. I'm simply doing a quality control check." The words buzzed against my skin while his hands roved across my thighs, playing with the edges of my panties as I pulled his mouth back to mine.

"I don't think taking your time teasing me is conducive to a quickie by the creek."

He swallowed my words as I spoke them.

"You're probably right." In a flash, Paxton entered me, and the shock quickly became pleasure. Pleasure I thought I'd never experience again, after what had happened over the past few days.

It was unbearable, knowing I'd almost lost this. I wrapped my arms around his neck, pulling him into an embrace. His quickened pace slowed down until the grind of our bodies built up the heat I'd come to expect around him.

"I don't want to lose this," I gasped into his ear as he continued the steady pace. "Not now that I know what's between us, and how I've always felt about you."

He bit into my neck as his breathing accelerated. His hands threaded through my hair. He pulled back and stared into my eyes with a fierceness I'd never seen before.

"How have you always felt about me, Rogers?"

Despite the situation we were in, the years of uncertainty, the lies I'd told myself, I owed him the truth, but I was Rose Rogers, and nothing could be that easy. "You already know."

"I want to hear you say it. I want to hear you say the words I never thought I'd ever hear from you."

He pulled out of me for a brief moment before he sunk back inside, causing me to stifle a cry of pleasure.

"You're … cruel," I groaned.

"So are you." He moved again, touching the exact spot that started my body quivering. "Say it."

I locked eyes with him, almost tempted to bury my face in his neck and refuse to speak. Instead, I said, "I love you."

"Finally. I think deep inside, I always knew."

My eyes widened. "But you don't love—"

"But I do love you, you idiot," he growled, his mouth back

on mine before I could say anything else. "Always have, and it scared me into silence."

"I'll never tire of hearing it." Those were the last words we spoke. The next few moments were spent listening to our bodies. The pent-up desire from years of unleashed passion flowed forward. Paxton picked up the pace, his body pressing into mine, his rhythm unwavering until I shook and shuddered in his arms. There was no question I belonged to him. I always had.

When we were finished, he glanced at his sopping wet clothes and breathed heavily against my neck.

"I think people might work out what happened."

I laughed softly. "Maybe, but I don't care."

His brow disappeared beneath the sweep of his bangs. "No?"

I pulled him back to me. "Now, they'll know you're mine."

He smiled. "I think I've always been, don't you?"

It was absurd to hear it, but it was true.

"Yes, and I've always been yours."

CHAPTER TWENTY-FIVE

PAXTON

It had been a tumultuous few days, but today was the wedding, and there wasn't a dark cloud hovering anywhere.

It seemed ridiculous that only yesterday, I dreaded the ceremony. I hadn't been likely to find it in me to be happy for my older brother, all things considered, but then everything changed.

The new reality couldn't be further from the truth. I was ecstatic for Owen—the first one of the Cooper brothers to finally bring a woman into the family, and I was happier for myself with Rose on my arm.

No matter what had happened over the last few days, we'd worked it out. More than worked it out. Everything between us was finally set free. We'd come to terms with who we were and who we are. How could I ask for more than that?

The happily married couple were on the stage, ready to dance their first dance. Just yesterday, I'd made love to Rose only a few feet away. I couldn't help but grin.

I glanced at her, expecting her to be thinking the same

thing, but her eyes were on Nick, then Rich, and then Nick again.

"What's wrong?" I asked.

She looked at me. "Nothing." She jumped up and down. "Look."

My eyes went straight to the table where Rich and Nick sat, hands entwined. "Who knew?"

Nick looked at us and smiled.

"He did. I swear he's years ahead of the damn curve. He came to Frazier Falls and found exactly what he was looking for."

We turned away from the scene, not quite sure what to say or do.

"You never had to leave to have what you wanted." I pressed my lips against hers in a soft, sweet kiss.

"Are we a train wreck waiting to happen?" The music started, and we swayed against each other from the sidelines watching Owen twirl Carl around the dance floor.

"It's not something I'm going to dwell on. Even if we are, no one can ignore a train wreck."

She laughed. She slid her hand down my arm to interlace our fingers.

"Care to dance?" she asked.

I nodded. "I'd love to." Having her in my arms was heaven, but not once had I had her in my bed.

We moved around the dance floor until I'd guided her to the exit.

"Where are you taking me?"

"How long do you think we can disappear before we're noticed?"

She studied the crowd in front of us. "A week?"

"I like the way you think." I tugged her behind me and rushed toward the creek. The soft pink fabric of her gown swished in the breeze as we raced up the path to my place.

CHAPTER TWENTY-SIX

ROSE - TWO YEARS LATER

"Are you ready?" Paxton asked.

"Am I the bridesmaid or best woman?"

"Hell if I know," he said. "How can you label what we are?"

"Easy, we're perfect for each other." I looked at my sparkling diamond ring. The one Pax put on my finger less than a month after Carla and Owen's wedding. I'd gone back to New York, but even a day without him was too much. I was no longer an editor at Flair but an independent consultant. I was also a wife and mother to a beautiful boy named Forest, who looked exactly like his father.

We stood at the edge of the creek and waited for Nick, who wore a custom Tom Ford tuxedo to walk up the aisle to Rich, who he'd dressed in Armani. No two men had ever looked so handsome and ready to start their lives together.

When Rich reached me, he stopped and smiled. "You're the nicest mean girl I've ever known."

I straightened his tie and gave him a hug. "Go find your bliss."

The people around us made our lives full. We'd all been

through hell and back. Carla and Rich almost lost their mill. Owen battled with anxiety and his health. Eli and Emily came close to losing their nerve, but Eli managed to get her to say I do after a trip to Vegas and a half dozen vodka cranberries. Paxton and I nearly lost each other because of words spoken and words withheld.

As I watched my best friend take his vows, I thought about the words Paxton and I had said to each other. We'd exchanged all the normal verses. The honor and cherish and death do us part, but we added a few at the end.

We promised that when we spoke, we'd always ask ourselves, *Is it true? Is it necessary? Is it kind?*

Words are powerful. They can break hearts and heal wounds. They start and end wars. They're necessary unless they're not. That was the biggest lesson I'd learned from my husband. He didn't waste words on people who didn't deserve them. Sometimes the most powerful thing to say was nothing at all. Thankfully, I'd become worthy of his love because ever since I said I do, he hadn't shut up.

"How long do you think we have to stay to make sure no one misses us?" Pax asked.

I knew where he was going. Mom was taking care of Forest, which left us free to be alone.

"We should wait until they say I do, don't you think?"

He frowned. "Fine, but not a minute more. What do you think of a girl named Creek?"

I bumped him with my hip. "You're all words and no action."

His frown changed to a slow, sexy grin. "I don't need words for the action I have in mind."

A SNEAK PEEK INTO A TABLESPOON OF TEMPTATION
DANIELLE

Danielle Morgan needed more than one breath of courage to exit her SUV. Today she needed two. There was no telling what waited beyond Trish's door. Last weekend it was Gene Horowitz; Danielle's surprise blind date. A date she was not prepared for.

Two weeks ago, she walked in on kitchen sexy time between Trish and her husband Rob testing out the strength of their new granite island. Right then, she vowed to never eat at Trish's unless it was takeout that went straight from the delivery person's hands to the coffee table.

Before Danielle could knock, her best friend opened the door and greeted her with a big smile. It was her I've-got-something-up-my-sleeve look.

"You better not have another one of Rob's cousins waiting for me." She turned, thinking she still had time to get away, but Trish took her elbow and pulled her inside.

"No one's here but Rob."

"Is he decent?" Danielle cleared her throat. "Meaning, is he dressed?"

Trish laughed. "Decent ... no. Fully clothed ... you bet."

Thank the heavens because there wasn't enough bleach to get that kitchen scene washed from her memory.

"You ready to go?" Trish picked up her purse from the hall table and looked over her shoulder. "Honey, I'm leaving."

Rob rushed around the corner and kissed her long and hard.

"It's not like she'll disappear forever. We're only hanging out for a few hours." Since her bestie had found love, their girl time shrunk from several nights a week dining out and watching movies to a few hours on the weekend. She didn't begrudge Trish's happiness. It was simply that Danielle was lonely. She wanted love. Instead, she got visiting rights to Trish.

She spun around and left the lovebirds on the doorstep to say their goodbyes.

Back behind the steering wheel, she waited and waited and waited.

Five minutes later, Trish skipped down the walkway like a teen after a tryst at Lookout Point. Her lips were red and bee-stung while her cheeks heated with a rosy blush.

"Sorry about that. It's a special day—our three-month anniversary."

Danielle rolled her eyes. "Tell me it's special when you hit your three-year anniversary. I hope his kisses still make you weak in the knees."

Trish dismissed her with a wave of her hand. "You're so jaded."

"I'm allowed to be." She squeezed the steering wheel harder and watched the blood drain from her fingers. "Don't forget that on my three-month anniversary, my husband wasn't running to give me a kiss. He was in room 301 banging Ms. Bancroft."

"Not all men are like Chris."

Danielle looked at her blissfully happy friend. "You're

A SNEAK PEEK INTO A TABLESPOON OF TEMPTATION

right. I can't punish every man for his infidelity, or his stupidity, or his complete disregard for anyone but himself. I should blame myself for being so impulsive. Who marries a guy after a month of dating?"

"We do. And sometimes it works out." She cocked her head to the side. "Look at Cinderella. She got the prince after one dance, and one day you'll hear the name Chris and say, 'Who'?"

"Let's hope." Seeing Trish happily married made Danielle happy, but it also made her miss the times when there was a man to warm her heart and her bed. "What are we doing today?" She pressed the ignition button, and her car purred to life.

"It's Swap Meet Saturday in Cedar Bluff." Trish bounced in her seat like a kid with front row seats to her favorite band.

"Thank God, I feared you'd set up another intervention."

Trish twisted to look at her. "Gene wasn't an intervention. He was a—"

"A disaster. The man wouldn't even look me in the eye, and you know how I feel about that. It's a sign of disrespect or dishonesty. Besides, he had bigger breasts than me."

"I can't speak to the man boobs, but Gene is shy, not dishonest."

"They say the eyes are the windows to the soul, and since I never saw his, I'm certain he's soulless." She drove out of Trish's neighborhood and turned onto the highway to Cedar Bluff.

"He's got a soul. He also has an astigmatism and that makes him self-conscious."

"Too bad he didn't have another *ism* like magnetism. The man was as exciting as a wet sponge. If this is what my dating life will be like, I'll pass. How could you think I'd be interested in him?"

A SNEAK PEEK INTO A TABLESPOON OF TEMPTATION

Trish let out an exasperated breath. "You're going to give me an aneurysm with your criticism. Cut me some slack. I'd never met him, but Rob said he was nice and decent looking."

"If you like trolls."

"Okay, I promise no more blind dates."

They pulled into the parking lot of Cedar Bluff High School and exited the car. "You need to promise to stop meddling in my life," Danielle said.

"You don't have one unless you call working around the clock a life. You never take time for fun. You know what they say … all work and no play—"

"Keeps me out of bankruptcy. I'm saddled with debt, and fun doesn't pay the bills."

"Fine. What's happening with the big takeover?"

"Argh, they're starting with the sweeping changes already—instead of The Pines, it's called Luxe Resorts."

"Ooh, sounds posh."

They entered the flea market and walked down the first aisle.

"Sounds scary to me. First, the name goes and next, the staff."

"You're good at your job. I don't imagine you'll have much to worry about."

Trish would never understand financial fear. She came from money.

Something caught Trish's eye, and she took off like a dog after a bone.

Danielle chased her, grateful she dressed in sneakers and jeans. "What are you looking for?"

"Inspiration." She held up a lamp with a shade faded by age and bartered with the owner until she got him to take five dollars. After the deal wrapped up, she asked him to hold it until she finished her rounds.

At the next vendor, Danielle picked up a heart-shaped

box and opened it to find nothing but lint and dust. Would her hollowed-out heart look the same inside?

Trish snatched the box from her and set it down, leading her to the next seller who had cross stitch and paint by number kits by the hundreds.

"You're thirty-five, not dead. Look at me." She stomped her foot to get Danielle's attention. "I found love in my thirties."

"I found it too, and all it got me was an empty bank account and heartache."

Trish lifted a cross-stitch of a lady surrounded by cats. "If you're not careful, you'll be her."

Danielle plucked the kit from her friend's hand and set it down. "Never. I'm allergic to cats. I'm good with my life the way it is."

"You work and sleep." Trish shook her head and moved them along.

"And take field trips with you, which is all the fun I can handle."

"Your life should be more. Maybe a hobby would be good." Trish turned around and headed back to the craft table. "Cross-stitch could be fun."

Had her life turned into TV dinners, cross-stitch, and *Murder She Wrote*? She'd only started watching that show to see if she could figure out a way to murder Chris and get away with it. But she realized the killer always got caught.

"If I agree to try a new hobby, will you stop setting me up with trolls?"

Smiling, Trish said, "Yes."

Danielle searched the nearby vendors for anything to get Trish off her back. Spotting a box of cookbooks with a five-dollar tag, she hurried over. Trish knew Danielle couldn't boil an egg, so it was a believable attempt at a hobby.

A SNEAK PEEK INTO A TABLESPOON OF TEMPTATION

"I'm getting this." Feeling victorious, she paid for the books and smirked.

Trish picked up the top one. *"The Beginners Guide to Baking."* She let out a laugh that shook her entire body. "I can't wait. The last time you "baked" a cake it cost you fifty dollars from Connie's confections."

"There was no way I was showing up empty-handed, and no one needed to know I bought that cake."

"My mom still thinks you're the most skilled cake baker in Pitkin County."

Danielle lifted her chin. "What they don't know won't hurt me." She asked the man to hold them, and they moved down the aisle. She had no intention of using the cookbooks. Chances were, they'd stay in the back of her car until she could donate them to a charity.

"I want to taste the first thing you cook. Rob can be your guinea pig too."

Danielle stopped to look at her friend. "Do you have a death wish? Besides, I thought you liked your husband."

"I do, but to keep you honest, I'll be your first taste tester. And you're not allowed to leave the books in the back of your SUV or give them away. Try your new hobby." With that, Trish raced to another table and picked up a chinoiserie bowl.

When she caught up with her friend, Danielle said, "You already have one like that."

"I did." She shrugged. "But you know … there are so many surfaces."

"That's why you needed that lamp." Danielle's jaw dropped. "Come to think of it, that entry table is new too. You two are disgusting."

"You're jealous."

She sucked in a breath and let out a sigh. "You're right." She moved through the rows. "Is it really that good?"

"What? The sex?" Trish turned and headed down the next aisle. "Remember that better-than-sex, chocolate cake Ms. Ferguson made?"

Danielle gasped. "No. Better than that?" That cake was an orgasm without a man.

"It's ten times that."

She shouldered her friend. "I would hate you if I didn't love you so much." Trish was the sister she always wanted, but not one of the two she had by blood. They met their freshman year of college and were inseparable. Trish's family was much like her own, except Danielle's father never wore a yarmulke and he ate bacon and pork ribs like they were the only meat in the world.

"And because you love me, you'll keep an open mind when I tell you what I did?" Trish led her to the funnel cake booth and ordered two with extra sugar.

"If it needs extra sugar, then it's got to be bad." She clenched her jaw until her teeth hurt. "What did you do?"

Trish picked up a funnel cake and stepped back. "It's not *that* bad."

"If you're buying sweets, it's bad. You also gave yourself running room, which means it's worse than bad. Spill it."

Trish stepped back once more. "I worked it out so you have an appointment with Aunt Freida."

Danielle's mind raced through Trish's relatives until she figured out who Freida was.

"You did not." She took a large bite of the sugary cake trying to cover the bitter taste in her mouth. "Aunt Freida, the matchmaker?"

"Yes, she set up my parents and my sister and my brother. She has a sixty percent success rate with women on the shelf."

Danielle choked, and a puff of sugar floated around them. "I'm not on the shelf. I'm only thirty-five."

Trish smiled. "My point exactly."

"Hey, you just promised no more set-ups if I agreed to try a hobby."

"No, I said no more trolls. Aunt Freida's got stellar taste. She'll find you a good man." With a flick of her finger, Trish removed the excess sugar from her plate, and they were once again surrounded by a sweet cloud. "She's expecting you tomorrow at noon. I'll text you her address. Keep in mind, she never works on Sunday, but you're family."

"No, no, no, I can't have your family setting me up. I'm not …"

Trish lifted her perfectly plucked brow. "Jewish?"

"No. You know race, religion, and status mean nothing to me. I want to find love organically. It shouldn't be a business deal."

Trish let out a huff. "With a marriage failure rate of fifty percent, why wouldn't you enter it like a business deal?"

"Did you and Rob enter matrimony with an outlined contract?"

"Yes, but it was verbal. I told him if he ever made me unhappy, I'd kill him." She cocked her head and grinned.

"I can show you some episodes of *Murder, She Wrote* that might come in handy. As long as Angela Lansbury doesn't show up, you should be fine."

They walked the rest of the way through the market. Trish bought everything to do with baking. There were measuring spoons and cups, and an apron that said, *spooning leads to forking.*

She handed them to Danielle. "I'm supporting your new hobby."

Danielle suppressed a groan. Now she'd have to pull out a cookbook and attempt to make something that wouldn't kill them all.

"I'll invite you over for a scheduled poisoning soon."

They picked up their purchases and headed to the car. When they got back to Trish's house, she leaned over and gave Danielle a hug. "You're worthy of more than you got. Never forget that. There is a man looking for you."

"Should I hoist a flag that says, 'I'm over here?'"

"No, but don't be late to Aunt Freida's, or she might curse you instead of blessing you."

"I don't want to go. What if she says I'm hopeless?"

Trish gathered her purchases and climbed out of the SUV. "I'll help you buy some cats."

GET A FREE BOOK.

Go to www.authorkellycollins.com

ABOUT THE AUTHOR

International bestselling author of more than thirty novels, Kelly Collins writes with the intention of keeping love alive. Always a romantic, she blends real-life events with her vivid imagination to create characters and stories that lovers of contemporary romance, new adult, and romantic suspense will return to again and again.

For More Information
www.authorkellycollins.com
kelly@authorkellycollins.com

Printed in Great Britain
by Amazon